W9-BAN-664

SUMITRA'S STORY

Sumitra's Story

RUKSHANA SMITH

COWARD-McCANN, INC. NEW YORK

First American Edition 1983

Designed by Lucy Bitzer
First printing Printed in the United States of America
First published by The Bodley Head Ltd., London, England

Library of Congress Cataloging in Publication Data
Smith, Rukshana. Sumitra's story.
Summary: When her East Indian family is displaced
from its home in Uganda by the repressive Idi Amin
regime, and resettles in London, the eldest daughter
Sumitra is torn between two cultures.
[1. East Indians—Great Britain—Fiction.
2. Family life—Fiction. 3. Prejudices—Fiction] I. Title.
PZ7.S6584Su 1983 [Fic] 82-19794
ISBN 0-698-20579-0

CHAPTER I

The day before Aunt Leela got married, Mr. Patel took Sumitra to Kampala to buy fireworks. Bap always bought the fireworks. He had become something of an expert in staging a display. He knew the names of all the different brands and would spend hours poring over catalogs and working out dramatic color effects.

"It is so important," he told his daughter as the bus jolted on, "to provide the correct balance. Would you, for example, send up a Golden Glory after a Golden Peacock?"

"No, Bap," Sumitra answered dutifully, staring out of the dusty windows at the dry countryside.

"No!" echoed her father, pleased. "You need a Purple Plunderer, an Emerald Emperor, a Blue Bomber to give the right variety and atmosphere." He murmured the names of the fireworks again, savoring the sounds and the images they evoked. They conjured up visions of the Gujarat province where he had been born: temples, peacocks, flowers all touched with the hidden passion and mystery of India.

"And not only color, but pacing is important," he continued, underlining his message with an outstretched finger. "First a quick rocket, to lift the eyes, then an action firework exploding in the middle distance, then some firecrackers, for excitement!" Sumitra had heard it all before. She leaned back drowsily on the hard seat and let Bap ramble on.

There were five coins in her cotton purse and they rattled faintly every time the bus jolted over the bumpy road. She loved the long journey across the sunbaked land. They passed through villages where Indian women crouched outside the houses, making *chapatis* in the sun. They went by African townships where naked children shouted and played outside the huts. Occasionally, high on the hills, they caught a glimpse of the white homes of the British. Here and there waterfalls cascaded down the slopes, running into lakes in which African boys were bathing while women washed clothes.

Bap reread his well-thumbed brochure. "Scarlet Pimpernel, Amber Adventurer, Silver Streak," he intoned. He wanted the celebrations for his sister Leela to be a success.

Sumitra stirred. Glancing down at her, he saw she was asleep and shifted so he could put his arm around the child to stop her falling off the seat. As he did so, he thought how lovely she was. She was the most beautiful of his daughters, her skin smooth and golden brown, her dark hair soft and gleaming, and her eyes almond-shaped and almost black. At ten years old she was nearly a woman. Bap felt his heart miss a beat. Time and place were illusions. One minute a baby was born and the next, or so it seemed to him, dowry settlements were being discussed with a future son-in-law. He turned once more to his catalog, and spent the rest of the journey planning the fireworks display for Sumitra's own wedding.

Sumitra held his hand tightly as they got off the bus. The heat hit them in sticky waves. Everyone seemed to be shouting and running. Bap led her down the bustling streets, past old African women selling snacks from their stalls, and into a long, narrow, unlit shop.

"Olindo?" he called. There was a long silence. Then, "Well, well, well, well, well!" said a voice from the shadows. Sumitra was frightened. She could see no one. A very black man moved slowly into the main shop. He was so fat that, as he laughed a greeting, ripples spread slowly from his cheeks down to his stomach. The movement reminded her of a lake into which a pebble had been dropped. She stared, fascinated.

"*Jambo, effendi, jambo!* So this is your daughter!" said Mr.

Olindo, pinching her cheek. Giving her a packet of melting jelly babies, he turned to Bap and smiled. "Someone is getting married, yes?" and as Bap nodded he turned and began taking boxes down from the shelves. "We got some new products from America only last week. They ignite by a new technique. . . ." Sumitra found the Swahili hard to follow. She went to the door and, sitting down on an old tin box, watched the activity outside.

She popped a jelly baby into her mouth. Sucking helped her to think. She wondered why black people spoke Swahili and Indians spoke Gujarati or Hindi. She wondered why some people were black, some brown, some white. She couldn't ask her father—he didn't like discussing things like that. In fact, although their house was always full of people, there was no one to whom she could really talk.

Mai was always busy entertaining friends or looking after Bimla and Ela. Sandya was only eight, too young to think about these things. She instinctively knew that she couldn't ask Cooky or Yusuf, the houseboy, and Leela, the aunt who had lived with them since their grandfather had died and who might have been able to help her, was too excited about her coming wedding. Yet Sumitra wanted to know. She vaguely felt that if she could find the answer to the question of why people were different, she would have discovered the secret of the world.

"Mai says Africans are dirty, that we are not to play with black children. So why are we living here? Why did they leave India if they don't like the natives of this country?"

At school, most of the children were Indian. There were a few Africans and some British, but as the school was situated near the Indian township, the majority of the pupils were neighbors with whom Sumitra had grown up. Although they all played together at school, they only invited children of their own race home. So African skipped off with African, Indian with Indian, white with white.

Sumitra smiled to herself, watching an old African lady walking by with a sack of *couscous* on her head. The lady reminded her of Birungi's grandmother who sometimes waited outside the school. Birungi was great fun, she thought, popping another jelly baby into her mouth. She could spit as far as a boy, turn twenty cartwheels at a time, climb trees. She was the daughter of a chief and betrothed to the son of a magic man. This gave her a bewitching aura of mystery.

I wonder if they would let me ask Birungi home? she thought, feeling the sweet juice trickle down her throat. But she knew she would never ask. There was no one *to* ask. She looked in the bag, there was one jelly baby left. It was green. Sumitra was struck by a sudden thought. All the jelly babies had been different colors: orange, black, yellow, white and green. Yet they had all come from the same bag. Somewhere in the back of her stomach she felt that this thought had a great significance, but she could not be sure. She tucked it away in her mind for future reference.

Bap had finished his purchases. He had two large parcels to carry, which jostled and bumped together on the way to Sanghvi's store. Mr. Sanghvi came from the same town in the Gujarat. Every few weeks the families visited each other, and it was with pleasure and warmth that Mr. Sanghvi shouted, "*Kem cho?*" as they walked in. "*Kem cho*, Devendra? *Kem cho*, Sumitra? How you have grown! How are the other girls? How is Charulatah?" Mr. Sanghvi talked as rapidly as the rain dropping through a rusty roof in a sudden downpour. "Sit down, sit down, Talika will fetch tea." Waving Bap into a chair, he clapped his hands together.

While the two men gossiped, Sumitra stared at the chair. It looked strangely out of place in Mr. Sanghvi's untidy store. SANGHVI'S SENSATIONAL EASTERN EMPORIUM, best in East Africa for Oriental goods, was crammed with shelves on which stood boxes of spices, condiments, powders, sweetmeats and cakes. Packets of joss sticks, sandalwood, perfumes and material for saris tumbled over the floor, and in the middle of it all, as if shrugging its arms in despair at the mess, was this very ancient peeling mahogany armchair, on which Bap was now perched. One of the legs had been damaged, no one could remember how, and someone had nailed on a piece of orange box to strengthen it.

Talika sidled through the bead curtain at the back of the shop and took Sumitra into the kitchen. Talika was sixteen, and stayed home to look after the house. "Take cakes from the tin," she ordered, "and put them on the plates." She filled a pan and began making tea. As Sumitra took the coconut squares and riceballs from the wooden box that served as a cupboard, she looked at Talika from under her eyebrows. Maybe Talika knew the answers. She seemed different from everyone else. Her mother had died when she had been a baby, and, as an only child, she might have had time to think and understand.

"Talika," Sumitra began, "why are some people black, and others brown and others white?"

Talika laughed scornfully. "You think I know? Ask the guru!"

Sumitra sighed and put the sticky cakes on the chipped plate. Talika cast her a glance of sympathetic annoyance, as if she recognized a kindred spirit. She added bitterly, "One day, Lord Krishna was bored. So he threw some *ghee* and sugar and water into a pan and poured it out. The *ghee* was white and it came out first. The sugar was brown and it came out next. The pan was burnt and black and dirty, so he left it for his woman to wash!" Sumitra listened to Talika's angry voice, trying to fathom why she was so cross. "That is why whites are best, Indians are second best, and blacks are the lowest. And that is why women always have to do the washing up!"

"What do you mean, Talika?" Sumitra asked, puzzled.

"Be quiet, girl, and hurry up. You will see one day!"

Talika swept out into the shop with the tea, and Sumitra followed, carefully carrying the tray of cakes. She felt even more bewildered than ever.

Bap had bought spices and cakes, which stood in paper bags on the counter. Sumitra suddenly remembered that she had five coins to spend. Taking them from her purse, she asked Mr. Sanghvi for some sweets. Mr. Sanghvi poured sweets from a jar into a big bag. "There you are, girl. I am giving you a lot because you are so pretty. Don't forget about my nephew," he said to Bap. "He is going to get a scholarship, you know, very clever boy, probably be a doctor or lawyer or something, have big business, much money. He will need a wife in a few years' time." He nudged Bap, and Sumitra felt a sense of panic. Would she have to get married, too, like Leela?

"And remember also," continued Mr. Sanghvi, "Talika is getting married next month." Sumitra looked at Talika. The girl was standing stiff and taut like an overstrung sitar. "Yes, she is marrying Shah's boy, going to live near Jinja, help run tea shop. Very high-class!"

Bap finished his tea and stood up. "Come along, Sumitra, we must go home now." As they were being ushered out of the shop, Mr. Sanghvi talking all the while, Sumitra took a handful of sweets out of the bag and pushed them clumsily into Talika's hand.

Then they were out in the street again. The bus on the journey back was crowded with workers returning home. Dusk fell quickly, and soon the stars were dimly visible in the red sky. Smoke rose from the homesteads, and oil lamps flickered warmly from the doorways. Sumitra closed her eyes and fell asleep with the jolting of the bus.

CHAPTER II

Food! It was the mainstay—not so much of their lives but of their civilization. Guests had not merely to be fed, but saturated, with plate after steaming plate of soup, rice, *pooris*, *chapatis*, *samosas*, peas, potatoes, all cooked in succulent sauces and spiced to perfection. Biscuits, *chevra*, *penda*, *gulab jamun*, *barfi*, sticky sweets and candies were proffered and eaten till the men felt the buttons straining on their shirts and the women surreptitiously loosened their saris. Motiben, Mai and Cooky had been baking over the kitchen fires for weeks, storing the batches in old tins, in preparation for the wedding.

It was Sumitra's job to label the tins. At school they learned the Latin alphabet, the square solid ABC, but she wrote the labels in Gujarati, adding flourishes to the letters, choosing a different crayon for each label. The tins spread around her like rusting silver drums, then were filled with food and taken into the storeroom. Yusuf stacked them on the shelves, high off the ground, safe from scorpions and rats.

The musicians began to arrive and the girls ran in and out of the house carrying cushions into the grassy courtyard. Preparations went on late into the night, the musicians discussing which *ragas* they were to play, the servants of neighboring friends arriving to help. Bap arranged and rearranged the fireworks, writing out complicated lists and then, inspired by a new notion, crossing out what he had already decided and adding his latest idea. Mai and Cooky continued to bake as if they could not stop.

Throughout the day, relatives that had not been seen since the last celebration began to arrive; friends from other parts of Uganda came packed nine or ten to a car. Sumitra watched in amazement as people unfolded themselves from their vehicles.

It reminded her of a magician she had once seen in an English film, who had conjured more and more rabbits out of a hat. Each time she thought a car must surely be empty, another sleeping child would be pulled out, or an old man who had spent the journey squashed beneath a grandson would be eased out of his corner, creaking and groaning, but protesting that he was fine, fine.

There were hordes of children, all of whom had to be admired and petted. Sumitra dashed about the garden playing with her cousins Nalima and Sadna. Every now and again Mai would call to them to come and help, and they would rush, laughing, into the kitchen to carry out plates of food.

The astrologer had told them that dusk was an auspicious time for the wedding. Unfortunately, the guru was nowhere to be seen. The musicians played a few prayer tunes, more food was produced from the kitchen, and Yusuf was dispatched to see if the guru and the astrologer could be found.

"I hope he won't say that we must postpone the wedding until tomorrow," muttered Mai, "or till next month!"

Then Yusuf came hurrying back, looking important. "The guru is coming. His wagon broke down and he had to hire a horse. He will be here directly." A cheer went up from the crowd.

The astrologer arrived on a garlanded bullock led by a small boy. He was reading a three-year-old copy of the *Guardian* that someone had sent him long ago and which he kept for important public appearances. Nobody noticed that he was holding it upside down—but they saw that he was reading an English newspaper, and appreciated the honor that this learned man was paying them by attending their feast. He recast the horoscope while Bap slipped some coins into his hand. "The ceremony can begin at once," the wise man pronounced. Mai breathed a sigh of relief as she touched his feet in gratitude.

The ceremony duly commenced. Leela and her husband-to-be, Jayant, sat indoors on a raised wooden dais with the guru seated beside them. The shrine was filled with fresh nuts, flowers and sweetmeats and the wedding couple were daubed with sandalwood paste. Motiben, Jayant's mother, and his younger brother, Gopal, were in positions of honor at the front of the congregation. As hostess, Mai wove in and out with dishes of food, while Bap, who should have been sitting on the dais, was fussing about muttering, "Scarlet Pimpernel, Golden Delight," instead of praying, *"Hare Krishna, Hare Rama."*

After the ceremony, Sumitra ran up to Leela and whispered, "Bap is making a lovely fireworks display, just for you!"

Leela held her close and said sadly, "Oh, Sumitra, I will miss you very much!"

"But you will come and see us every day?" the child asked in surprise.

"No, my dear." Leela spoke softly. "Motiben has decided that we must go to live in England. Gopal is coming, too."

"England!" Sumitra echoed. "There are pictures of England in our readers. It is thousands of miles away, and cold and foggy. Why ever must you go there?"

Leela smiled, and then Sumitra heard her name being called. She was wanted in the kitchen.

The fireworks display was magnificent. Bap had excelled himself. The sky was a riot of purple, gold, green, amber and silver. Beyond the gates of their house, scores of small African children could be seen looking upward and marveling at the sight. The children of the guests ran excitedly through the garden *oohing* and *aahing* appreciatively and clapping after every bang. Following each round of applause, Bap raised his hands in acknowledgment like a seasoned impresario.

Before lighting the last firework, Bap turned to the crowd and spread his arms wide. The audience became quiet, hushed with expectancy. He lit the fuse; nothing happened. The Africans outside the gate jeered and scoffed. Cooky shouted at them in Swahili to go away. Bap tried again, and with a rush the firework ignited, shot up into the air and divided and subdivided into a myriad glowing sparks. "The Golden Emperor," Sumitra murmured, and, quoting from the catalog, added, "a splendid way to conclude your pyrotechnic performance!"

It *was* a beautiful finish. The sky was transformed into filigree patterns of burning light. Suddenly, one of the sparks deviated in a violent, erratic movement, freely winging up and round the sky.

As it swooped down, it seemed to Sumitra that it was aiming for her deliberately. It landed on her hand and scorched her skin. She screamed with pain, and was surrounded by fussing women. Cooky came running out with Tiger Balm, which was smeared on the blistered patch. Mai cradled her in her arms. Motiben fanned her cheeks with a banyan leaf.

"It is a good omen," laughed Bap, happily inventing an instant myth. "Hunuman was burned by a brand in the other world. It brings luck. It is a sign that this night is an auspicious one." Sumitra held back her tears. She was cosseted, bandaged, fed sticky *gulab* and told to rest.

"Lucky pig," Sandya whispered fiercely as she was upgraded to position of chief helper.

Sumitra now sat among the grown-ups, holding her bandaged hand carefully on her lap. Little Ela toddled over to her and sat on her knees, her head drooping onto Sumitra's shoulder. Half-dozing, Sumitra listened as the adults talked. She heard them speak of the president of India, of Uhuru, of England, of leaving Uganda. It didn't mean much to her, but she tried to remember phrases so that she could ask someone later.

The guests stayed for a week, and then the house was quiet. No more guests slept on the steps or in the kitchen. Grumbling, Cooky and Yusuf helped them clear up; the old dog took up his place again in the yard.

"Cooky," Sumitra asked, remembering a half-heard conversation in the garden, "what's a free canization?"

Cooky was beating out bedspreads and raising clouds of dust in the shafts of sunlight. She readjusted her cotton headscarf, and wiped the sweat from her face. "Why, child," she replied, "it's a canization you don't have to pay for!" She smote the cover again as if to signal the end of the discussion. "Now run along, girl, I'm busy!"

At school, Sumitra went down to the sand patch with Birungi. "Rungi, what's a free canization? I heard some people talking about it at Leela's wedding."

"*Africanization*, stupid! Africanization means that we Africans want to run our country. My father has told me about it. At present, the British run the schools and the law courts, Indians own businesses and shops, and the African labors. In future, we want to run the schools and shops as well as working."

"But what will the Indians and white people do?" Sumitra asked, puzzled. She had never thought that anything could be changed. Indeed she had never noticed the clear-cut divisions that Birungi had just mentioned. It had certainly never crossed her mind that, the way things were, they added up to one huge injustice. And she was part of that injustice. The thought shocked her, made her feel frightened.

"What will they do? I don't know!" Birungi said bluntly. She always told the truth.

Sumitra tried again. "Rungi, why are some people black and some white and some brown?"

"I don't know. I have often wondered this myself. Come on, let's practice cartwheels." They somersaulted on the stony sand until the teacher rang the bell and they trooped into school.

So, Birungi couldn't answer her question. Was there perhaps no answer? They opened Reader VI at page thirty-seven and listened to Miss Evans giving the lesson. The teacher was an Englishwoman on a V.S.O. mission. She had red hair that fell down her back in untidy curls, and pale, blotchy skin. She wore blouses and skirts and nylon stockings. The girls thought she was beautiful and very fashionable. Sumitra played with her plaits and wished her own hair were red. But Indians never had red hair.

" 'Mrs. Brown is taking Fred for a walk in the snow.' Who knows what snow is?" Sumitra knew that snow was white and sticky. It was rain that froze as it fell. One day her father had bought them a snow scene from Gulu market. It was a glass bubble enclosing a little girl and boy, and when it was shaken, white bits floated around in a snowstorm.

She tried to imagine Leela and Jayant in a snowstorm. Leela would have bits of snow stuck to her sari. It was two weeks since they had left with Motiben and Gopal to go to England, too soon to receive a letter. She wondered why they had left Uganda where it was hot and sunny and the days were a round of visits and excitement.

Most of what she knew about England had been gleaned either from the Cambridge Overseas Readers or from Jamin, an old man who had studied in England before the war. "England is an island in the western hemisphere." It was near a continent called Europe, which was a large landmass like Africa. There were lots of different countries, and tribes speaking different languages and with differing customs. Sometimes, as in Africa, the tribes fought.

But the geography and climate of Europe were quite different from those of Africa. England, Sumitra had learned, was a green land with grassy meadows through which brooks and rivers meandered. It was hard to imagine a green land far away. All Sumitra could do was to put English scenery into African contexts. Her fields and rivers were always bounded by sandy plains; her English-style houses perched on African hills.

One evening Jamin had come to visit Bap and, sitting cross-legged on the veranda, flexing his gnarled hands to pick out the pecan nuts, he had told them about people in England. All Englishmen, or all rich Englishmen at any rate, he said, wore bowler hats, and all English ladies drank tea. Englishwomen often wore scarves tucked about their heads, something like African women, and had an amazing habit of screwing their hair into paper twists or sometimes iron pegs, in order to make their hair as frizzy as the hair of the Acholi.

Miss Evans rang the bell for lunch. Sumitra stopped wondering how anyone could screw their hair into paper twists and ran into the sandy playground with Birungi and Mary. As usual, the three girls divided up their lunch packets and shared them around. Mary had brought egg sandwiches, Rungi had a pot of *mealie* and beans, and Sumitra unwrapped *chapatis* and potato with mustard seed.

"I'm not allowed to eat eggs today," Sumitra announced cheerfully, tucking hungrily into Mary's sandwiches.

"Why not?" asked the other two.

"I don't really know—it's something to do with Lord Krishna, but I can't remember why."

"We're leaving soon," Mary told them, taking a *chapati* and dipping it into Rungi's beans.

"Where are you going?" asked Rungi.

"To England."

"England! That's where my aunt has gone!" cried Sumitra in astonishment. "She's gone to London. Where will you go? Why are you going?"

Mary shook her fair hair off her tanned face. "Dad only told us last night," she said. "We're going to Manchester. That's in the north of England where my parents come from. I've never been there—I don't think I'll like it. I like it here." She looked very sad, and as they watched her they saw she was crying. Rungi and Sumitra put their arms around her, and tried to comfort her.

"Here, have some *penda*."

"Try a *mealie*, you know you love *mealies*."

"Dad says we better go now, before we're kicked out!"

"But who can kick you out?" asked Sumitra in surprise. "You're white."

"My dad says that President Amin is going to throw out all the British, even the engineers like him. So we must go before there's trouble."

"What trouble?" Sumitra asked anxiously.

"Oh, I don't know." Mary sounded tired. "You know how grown-ups go on. You can't ask them what they mean or they'll stop talking about it until you've gone to bed. Anyway, I'll miss you two so much. Will you write to me?"

"Of course we will!" said Birungi. Then she added with a grin, "It's not us you'll miss, it's the delicious food!"

Mary jumped on her friend and started to tickle her. Sumitra sat in the sand, drawing the Latin alphabet in the dust. Trouble, Mary had said. It was true, there was a feeling in the air, a tension, an excitement, an underlying current of change that pulsed through the heat, waving in a shaky haze over the sparse grass. She smiled through her panic. She felt as if she were one of the figures in the glass bubble Bap had bought. It was being shaken and she had no control over the events that were blizzarding around her.

CHAPTER III

For some time Sumitra had been aware that adult conversations suddenly came to a halt when she or Sandya entered a room. Yet if the girls sat quietly and the grown-ups forgot they were there, talk would revolve around the events erupting in Uganda.

After a few more months, all reticence in front of the children had been abandoned. It was useless for Bap and Mai to pretend that nothing was happening. Whole families of friends had emigrated to Britain, to America, to India. Indians were being dispossessed; their shops and businesses were given to Africans. The teachers at school were black now, and the Indian children stayed at home. They stayed at home because of their parents' prejudice and their own fear. To venture out meant risking violence, shooting, death. Uganda was on the march to freedom and *dunkanwallahs*, petty shopkeepers, had no place in the glorious revolution.

Cooky had gone. Yusuf and the dog moped around. Mai was cross, tearful. "Pack up! Pack up!" she kept screaming, but the girls did not know what to pack. "Leave the saris, just take what we need. Leave Bap's sitar. Just take a few clothes. Hurry, hurry!"

So they packed, a girl of eleven and a girl of nine, not knowing where they were going, nor why, nor how long for. They packed in a state of numbed shock. Leela had now been gone for a year. During that time Idi Amin had been making speeches against the Asian community and threatening to kick them out. That was why Bap was now queuing in the heat for the papers to enable them to leave. He had been gone for three days, the queue hardly moving. Twice a day Mai went to the British Embassy to take him food.

Once she had taken Bimla with her. They had seen dead men in the streets. Now Bimla was lying on her pallet in a fever, shouting, "Shot, shot!" It was like a nightmare, Sumitra thought, as they filled cases with religious pictures and ornaments, and boxes with clothes and household goods. As each box was filled, Yusuf hammered it down, tears streaming from his eyes. Sumitra painted Leela's address in black ink on the pale wood.

"Where are we going?" asked Sandya. "Are we going to India?"

"No, we're going to England," Sumitra sobbed.

"But you are the only one who can speak English properly! What shall we do there? I don't want to go. I shall stay here. I like it here." The two girls threw their arms round each other and wept.

Mai burst into the room with another pile of clothes. "Hurry, hurry!" she screamed, her voice tense with fear. Then she saw they were crying. "Now, now, my dears, please don't cry. We have to go. There is no choice. The president has told all Indians to leave Uganda. It is better to go than to be hanged. We will go to Leela's house. If we stay here, we will be killed."

Sumitra looked at her mother. Mai's face was streaked with tears and her hair was untidy. Her sari was crumpled and stained. It was then that Sumitra realized that the nightmare was real. The things that were happening in the streets, the distant gunfire and the moans, these had not affected her. But the sight of her usually calm, elegant mother now creased and grimy told her that their former life was at an end.

"Why can't we go to India, Mai?" Sandya was asking. "After all, you always tell us that we are Indian. We speak Gujarati, we know Indian customs. I don't want to go to England!"

"That is enough!" Mai snapped. "It is lucky we have British passports. There you will get good schooling, free! You don't know what you are saying! We cannot take any money with us. How could we live in India? In England we will get a house, you will go to school. Now hurry, hurry!"

They went on wrapping plates and packing clothes. Sumitra looked again at her mother. It was true that Mai had always been a good manager, but they had never realized that Cooky and Yusuf had done most of the work. Life during this last week had been an unending muddle. Meals had been missed, even when they had managed to procure any food. Mai had almost forgotten how to cook and shop without the help of servants, and none of the girls had ever needed to learn. Sumitra wondered what life would be like in England, if they would have servants there.

There was no more time for wondering. Bap came back with Mr. Sanghvi and the passports, and the news that the next plane was leaving in twenty minutes. They gathered up what they could and told Yusuf to send their luggage to the address marked on the boxes. Bap gave him the remainder of his Ugandan currency and the dog, then they piled into Mr. Sanghvi's car and were off. Yusuf wept. The dog howled. Even the mango tree looked sad. They all tried to avoid looking at the dead bodies hanging like rotten fruit from the trees. Sumitra cried as she thought of all the friends she would never see again, Cooky, Yusuf, Birungi. "*Kwa heri ya kuona,*" Yusuf had said to them as they left. "Until we meet again!" But she knew that they would never meet again.

The plane was full of weeping, bewildered Indians. "Yes, my friends," said Mr. Sanghvi, "we have worked hard to plant the tree and now others will reap the fruit!" He looked round prophetically, wagging his head and looking pundit-wise. Sumitra thought of the mango tree in the garden. She didn't mind if Yusuf ate the fruit. She hoped he would be all right—he might get shot for having worked for them. She resolved to write and ask him how he was at the earliest opportunity.

Bap sat upright and taciturn. He had gone to Uganda as a

young man, as an Englishman might go to America, full of ambition and initiative. He had worked hard and built up a flourishing business. He was known and respected in his village, his house was fine and sturdy. Now he was going with his wife and four daughters to a country whose civilization he was meeting for the first time thanks to British Airways.

As the plane flew steadily onward, the mood of the passengers changed. Worried and frightened as they were, they now felt safe for the first time in months. Women opened packages out of which emerged *samosas, penda, chevra.* Plastic drink-bottles appeared and friends and families exchanged delicacies. The exodus had become a picnic, an adventure. The hostesses brought round the statutory meals—these were politely accepted and left to congeal in cold messes on the plates. Bimla was convinced that the airline food had been poisoned by the Africans, but happily ate seven homemade *samosas.* Ela was sick. Women fussed over her, bringing out ointments, medicines, talismans.

Sumitra tried to understand the English of the air hostesses. Up to then, the only English she had heard had been the English of Miss Evans. Miss Evans had always spoken slowly and clearly, repeating difficult words, phrasing questions in a way that she knew the class would understand.

Gradually the passengers fell asleep. The air hostesses and stewards quietly removed the dishes, folded up tables, brought blankets and switched off the main lights. In a half-dream, Sumitra smiled sleepily at one hostess. The girl, a tall blonde with a kind face, smiled back and patted her kindly on the shoulder. "I shall be an air hostess when I am grown up," Sumitra decided. "That is what I shall be."

They woke to the sound of the captain's voice. "We are now flying over France. We shall be landing at Heathrow in thirty minutes."

"*Su che? Su che?*" demanded a hundred voices, and those

who had understood relayed the message. Damp cloths came out of the bags, faces were wiped, hair brushed, saris tidied.

"Ela is three years old. Her sister Bimla is five. Sandya is nine and Sumitra is eleven. Sumitra is the oldest. Ela is the youngest. They are flying in an airplane." Sumitra had to interrupt her English lesson because of the crackly announcement. "Fasten your safety belts, please. We are at London Heathrow." The plane settled into a gradual decline and gently bumped on the tarmac.

Thanks to Cambridge Reader VI, Sumitra became the acting head of the family. As the only fluent English speaker, it fell to her to organize, interpret, explain and decide. At the age of eleven she became the form-filler, the provider, the decision-maker. Bap, finding that the role he had filled for so many years was no longer his, went into a deep depression. He sat on his bed in the men's dormitory, looking out at the English autumn.

Mai and the other women cooked the food in the communal kitchens of the hastily converted army barracks. Sandya was busy looking after Bimla. The child was still in a state of terror, frightened by every sound. Again and again she muttered, "I hate President Amin! I hate President Amin!"

Sumitra filled in forms. "Surname: Patel. Head of household: Devendra Patel. Age: 38. Spouse:" Here she had to stop and look up in her dictionary. Spouse—Husband or wife, from O.F. spous (masc.) spuse (fem.). "Charulatah Patel. Age: 30. Names and ages of children: Sumitra Patel—11. Sandya Patel—9. Bimla Patel—5. Ela Patel—3. Residence required in: London."

All the refugees wrote down London or Birmingham or Leicester, unaware that they were being encouraged to "disperse." Bap and Mai did not know that the British saw them as a threat, part of a huge wave of immigrants speaking a different language, wearing exotic clothes, worshiping strange gods. At the same time, Bap and Mai felt frightened by a culture that seemed to them brazen and brash. The authorities tried to ease the situation by spreading the immigrants around the country. But the immigrants did not want to go to Scotland or Wales. "Scotland? Where is Scotland?" Mai asked. "Where is it? Leela will come and get us, don't worry, she will come. We will live in London."

London had a comforting sound. It was a name they all knew. They had heard it on the news; they had read the name in the papers. But if someone had taken them to Glasgow and told them it was London, they would have been perfectly happy. It was not to London the place they wanted to go, after all, everything was so different and strange. It was to London the sound.

"Religion: Hindu. Occupation of head of household: Owner of radio shop in Uganda. Languages spoken by head of household: Gujarati, Hindi, Swahili."

They spent fourteen days in the camp, getting acclimatized. The weather was cool but sunny, what the English called an Indian summer. Bap slowly began to revive. They sat together at the long tables and ate the meals. Occasionally social workers and volunteers came and talked to them, taking the older women off to teach them English, or to show them how to use the telephone. They went into the post office, round the shops, visited the hospital. The women came back laughing and confused. People had stared at them, children had called out. The Englishwomen were wearing short dresses, cut low at the necks. Shops were filled with strange clothes and shoes and food. There were order and straight lines everywhere. Shops specialized in one thing, fruit or meat or packaged food, instead of selling wares in the tumbling profusion and muddle that they had assumed was the norm. The houses were in lines, each with a garden with orderly flowers.

"Next of kin in Great Britain: Mr. Jayant Patel. Worthington Avenue, Highgate, London."

Jayant was trying to find the family. Bap had been unable to let him know when they were leaving, and had written a letter on arriving in England. But he had not known the address of the camp, so Jayant spent days phoning up relief organizations and asking where his family had been sent.

Every night, before she went to sleep, Sumitra said to herself, "I know Leela will come tomorrow. I know Leela will come tomorrow." Then she would stare wakefully at the whitewashed ceiling and look around to see if Mai and her sisters were asleep. Mai was usually lying huddled under the coverlet. Ela and Bimla shared a bed—Ela would be asleep, her chubby arm dangling on the floor. Bimla was mumbling the old litany, "I hate President Amin! I hate President Amin!" Sandya would be dozing, tired out with the effort of practicing English. Sumitra would watch the moonlight flickering in the windows.

She was still trying to understand the new balance of her life. In Uganda they had been brown, therefore beneath the British but above the natives. They had lived a privileged life compared to the majority of Africans. But now, they were no longer high up in the pecking order, but low down. Once again it seemed to be the old question: different colors, different languages, different cultures, different rewards. But why, why, why? She fell asleep, dreaming of Birungi and of Yusuf. Rungi was sitting under the mango tree in their garden, while Yusuf fanned her face.

CHAPTER IV

Someone had been tampering with the clocks. Every time she looked up, expecting to find that at least two hours had passed, Sumitra found that only half an hour had gone by. Unused as she was to the long English evenings, the empty days seemed to move as slowly as a snail crawling up a wall. The army camp was emptying now; relatives or friends of the refugees came to claim their families like people collecting packages from a Lost Property Office.

One afternoon she watched idly as two figures got out of a car, looked around the barracks and then walked slowly up the drive. "I wonder who will be leaving today?" she said to Mai, who was sitting beside her in the Officers' Mess, busily sewing a dress for Ela. Then with a sudden scream of recognition, she jumped out of her seat, laughing and crying at once.

Mai looked up, alarmed. "It's Leela!" shouted Sumitra. "Leela and Jayant. They've come to get us at last!" Mai rushed out of the Mess to fetch Bap and the children. Sumitra ran sobbing into Leela's arms as the newcomers came into the entrance hall. "Leela, Leela, I knew you'd come. We've waited so long, but I knew you'd come." She took them into the Mess and the rest of the family came in, all talking at once, hugging and smiling and weeping with relief.

Their few personal belongings were soon packed into bags and they piled into Jayant's car. "It's a new car," he said proudly, and Bap walked around it as Jayant pointed out the windshield wipers, the self-locking doors, the capacious trunk. Then with an important roaring of the engine, a screeching of wheels on gravel, they were off, too excited to feel squashed. The adults exchanged news, while the girls stared out of the windows, exclaiming at each new sight. "Look, Mai, look, the cows are so fat! And the horses and sheep, see!" They marveled at the congested roads, laughed at the short-skirted girls, admired the green countryside.

As they drove through London, Jayant pointed out the sights. "This is Buckingham Palace where the queen lives. That is Hyde Park. This is Oxford Street where all the famous shops are." Then they were in the suburbs with pleasant tree-lined roads and solidly built houses. Jayant stopped the car outside one of them. "Here we are," he said, enjoying their admiration. "This is my house." Gopal and Motiben came running out, smiling broadly in welcome.

They tumbled out of the car and stretched cramped limbs. Bimla clung to Sumitra's hand. She had seen the white net curtains twitch in the window of the house next door. Mai shivered, although it was quite warm. "Come in, come in," urged Leela and Motiben, and the Patels were ushered into their new home.

Soon they were all sitting down, drinking tea and eating biscuits and cakes. Had it not been for Mai crying, Bimla whispering, "I hate President Amin!" and Bap's unusual quietness, it would have been like any afternoon back home.

Sleeping arrangements were quickly sorted out. Motiben, Leela, Jayant and Gopal occupied the upper floor, while the refugees slept on mattresses and settees in the living room and kitchen. This arrangement was perfectly acceptable to them all, as they came from a society in which rooms were flexible and adaptable. As yet, the concept of a dining room, living room, bedroom was new. All around them, neighbors slept in bedrooms, ate in dining rooms, cooked in kitchens, entertained in lounges. But having a family sleeping in every available room did not worry Motiben. It was normal. Only English social workers and journalists would have been horrified, Sumitra much later realized.

It soon became clear that life without a cook and a houseboy was very hard. Leela, Motiben and Mai spent much of their time in the kitchen, preparing delicious and elaborate dishes. Space was a convention that could be tampered with, but food most definitely was not. Convenience foods were an unknown, unwelcome concept.

The following day, Jayant took them around to "sort things out." They admired his easy English, the protective manner he adopted toward them, the way in which he spoke to the clerks at the Education Offices and the Employment Centre. By the end of the week he had found schools for the girls to attend, and a job for Bap.

In Uganda, Bap had owned a shop selling electrical goods and specializing in repairs. But in this cold new land, he was dumb—he could not speak English. He was to work in a factory a short bus ride away, making components. It was simple assembly work, but it was a job, and several other Uganda Asians worked there. Bap felt belittled by this prospect and became sullen and depressed.

There was a primary school not far from the house, where Sandya and Bimla were enrolled. Sumitra was to attend Northfields, a modern comprehensive in Finchley. The same thoughts went through all their minds. How would they manage with the language? Would they make friends? Would they be happy? They all envied little Ela who was playing happily in the garden, calling out to the birds in Gujarati and telling Indian fables to the next-door Siamese cat.

The Patels set off on Monday morning to their new worlds, like space travelers setting off for a new planet which had existed before their arrival but which they had never seen. Bimla and Sandya walked hand in hand down the road, looking back every few yards to see if Mai was still waving. They looked small, thin and scared.

Sumitra left early for Finchley. She followed the map that Jayant had drawn and found the school quite easily. It was enormous, far larger than anything she could have imagined. Their school at home would have fitted into one of the annexes. She walked around staring. It was made of glass and bricks, laid out in straight lines. Paths led from one complex to another. She looked at her watch. It was 8:30. Gangs of children were arriving, shouting and waving to each other.

One boy running by saw her standing, looking lost and lonely. "New girl?" he asked cheerfully. Sumitra nodded. The boy was tall and confident, and wore a yellow badge that read PREFECT. "Come on," he said, "I'll take you to the headmaster, Old Jonesy."

He strode off, and Sumitra tried to keep up with him. She felt shy, nervous and worried. She hated the new school uniform that Motiben had bought her. It felt stiff and cold and the points of her shirt collar dug into her skin. The boy was knocking at the headmaster's door. "Come in," said a deep voice. Sumitra stood motionless, suddenly trembling. The boy pushed her inside. "There's a new girl for you, Mr. Jones," he said. "Thank you, Paul. Run along now." Paul grinned at Sumitra and banged the door behind him, making the girl jump and drop her bag.

The headmaster got up from the desk where he had been sitting, shuffling through some papers. He was a kind-looking man with brown hair and blue eyes. Retrieving Sumitra's bag for her, he shook her hand and gestured to her to sit down. Then he pulled up another chair and sat down beside her.

"You must be Sumitra Patel. We are expecting you. We've put you in the first year, in Miss Watkins's class. I know that you must feel very strange at the moment–how long have you been in England?"

"Three weeks only," Sumitra whispered, tears welling up in her eyes.

"I realize that you need to work on your English and that life is most unsettled for you, but we will be patient with you if you work hard for us. Now I'll take you to your class and introduce you to the teacher."

He led her through countless corridors and up and down stairs, stopping outside a classroom marked 1C. He threw open the door and marched in. Sumitra followed timidly behind him, positioning herself so that the rest of the class could not see her. "Good morning, Miss Watkins," he said cheerfully. "This is Sumitra Patel, your new pupil." Turning to the girl and exposing her to the curious eyes of thirty students, he told her, "You know where my room is if you need any help." She did not know where his room was, had no idea how to get there in this maze of a place, but smiled politely and nodded.

Miss Watkins pushed back her blond hair and gave a welcoming smile. "What's your name again, dear?" she asked. "I didn't quite catch it."

Sumitra felt her heart beating really hard. She glanced down to see if her rib cage was shaking. It wasn't. "Sumitra," she said very softly, her eyes fixed on the shiny wooden floor. She suddenly remembered the sandy floor of her old school and felt very desolate.

Miss Watkins called to a small, dark-haired girl, "Hilary, I want you to look after Suma–Sutri–I'm sorry, dear, tell me again." Sumitra repeated her name, and she and Hilary exchanged smiles. "Help Su–her to settle in and feel at home," said Miss Watkins. Hilary moved up to let Sumitra sit down.

"Hi, what's your name again?" Sumitra got a pen and wrote her name on the back of Jayant's map. She wondered if Bap and her sisters were having the same trouble. Their names were so familiar and easy, it was hard to comprehend why these people were finding them so hard.

"Come on," said Hilary, getting up and pulling her new friend by the hand. "It's our turn for assembly today."

"What's that?"

"Don't you know what assembly is? You'll soon find out!"

They filed into a large hall smelling of polish, sweat and cabbage, and sat cross-legged on the floor. The walls were lined with bars and ropes. For one awful moment, Sumitra thought a recalcitrant pupil was going to be hanged, then she realized that the ropes must be used for climbing games. She felt conspicuous and kept her eyes on the ground, hiding her face behind her hair. The hall began to fill up. Sumitra had never seen so many children at once. They whispered and joked, pulling their friends' hair or slipping pellets of paper down backs, punching and pinching when the teachers weren't looking.

Cautiously, Sumitra looked around. The pupils were all different sizes, shapes and colors. About three-quarters were European, the rest seemed to be of West Indian, African, Chinese, Malaysian and Indian origin. Among the European faces, she could identify Greek, Spanish and Italian features. The whispering and giggling continued as the headmaster spoke about the love of God and they sang hymns to the music of a piano.

From what she could make out, they were praying to the god Jesus. Miss Evans had told them about him—Sumitra had understood that Jesus was similar to Lord Shiva, King of the Dance. Shiva's dance represented three things, while Jesus was a Trinity, three in one. Father, Son and Holy Ghost—Rhythm, Release, Heart of the Universe. As if to confirm her understanding, the teacher at the piano began to thump out "I am the Lord of the Dance said he."

"And now I want to welcome a new girl." Sumitra thought she was going to faint. She hoped he meant another new girl. "Will Sumitra Patel please stand up?" She sat immobile, her legs locked beneath her. "Come on, Sumitra," the headmaster said. Hilary gave her a poke and Sumitra stood up, while two hundred heads turned round to look at her. "Welcome to the lower school. We will all help you as much as we can. Now, everybody, rise!" Thankfully, she saw that all the students were getting up—she was no longer alone.

"Have you got your dinner money, dear?" Miss Watkins asked as they returned to the classroom.

Sumitra stared at her. What was this? She had some *chapatis* and *penda* in her bag, so what did the teacher mean? Hilary came to her rescue. "Have you any money?"

"My bus money, that is all."

Hilary spoke up. "Sumitra's only got enough money for her fare home. She probably forgot it."

Miss Watkins quickly wrote a note and sent someone to the office. "Bring it tomorrow, dear. I'll put some in for you for today."

No one at home had said anything about dinner money. Motiben and Leela had had nothing to do with schools, and they had all assumed that the girls would take a snack with them as usual. "How much shall I bring?" Sumitra asked Hilary. Hilary slapped her hand on her brow in mock despair. "Don't you know anything? It's seventy-five p. a week."

"Have you brought your shorts?" the teacher was asking.

Sumitra shook her head again. She hadn't brought anything she needed. They went out to change for games—Sumitra felt shy as the other girls peeled off their clothes and donned their sports gear. The teacher lent her a pair of baggy shorts and she hurriedly got changed. No one else seemed bothered about appearing half-naked in front of the boys, and it wasn't as embarrassing as having to stand up in the hall, so she tried to appear calm and assured. At least she knew how to play games and to run fast.

After school Miss Watkins called her. "Well, dear, how have you enjoyed your first day?"

Sumitra didn't know what to say, how to explain the strangeness, the informality, the different attitudes. She smiled shyly. "I liked it."

"You will need to work very hard. You have a lot of catching up to do, and the sooner your English improves the better it will be for you. I'll arrange for you to have remedial lessons instead of games for this term, and we'll see how it goes. You must borrow Hilary's books and copy up her notes for all the time you have missed. It will be a hard few months for you, but I'm sure you can cope. And it will be worth it in the end." She smiled encouragingly.

"Thank you, teacher." Sumitra ran to the bus stop, eager now to be home and see how the others had managed. Sandya and Bimla had not taken dinner money either. As the bus drove through the streets, she looked out at the brightly lit shops and thought about the confusing events at school. Hilary had promised to help her and had invited her to tea next week. She wondered if Bap would let her go.

Jumping off at her stop, she ran all the way to the house, her bag bumping against her side. She arrived home to find Bimla and Sandya in tears. They hadn't understood the teachers. Some children had called them "Blackie." They hadn't taken their dinner money. They didn't like school dinners, anyway, and they weren't going to school anymore. In the midst of all this commotion Bap came home. He was crosser than they had ever seen him before. Some men had jeered at him on the bus and called him a "Paki."

He asked Sumitra what this meant. She didn't know. Bap made her look it up. She opened the dictionary. "Park–a grassy space, large enclosed piece of ground." That didn't seem to apply. She found "Parky–chilly of air, morning etc. (etym. dub.)." This seemed equally mysterious. She tried once more. "Pack–bundle of things wrapped up for carrying (etym. ME packe, cf. Du. pak G. pak.)." They discussed these meanings, puzzled. Then Jayant returned home and explained.

Bap exploded. "Why, back home I was better than them! I had my own house, my own shop! Because they are white, they think they are better than me. We are better than them. Remember that, all of you, we are better than them! Look at them, letting their women run around half-clothed, irreligious meat-eaters, drunken people, ignorant men, loose women! Remember, children, we have a culture thousands of years old. We must be proud. Why, most of our greatest literature was written when the British were still living in caves! Do not forget that we are better than them, whatever they call us!"

The children were not likely to forget. They were to hear this diatribe at least once a week for the rest of their childhood.

More puzzled than ever, Sumitra helped prepare the meal. First they had been told to hate black people in Uganda, now they had to hate white people in England. But back in Uganda, white people had been honored and respected.

Somewhere at the back of her mind, something stirred. It was the answer to her question. It was there, within her, but as yet beyond her understanding.

CHAPTER V

The family was pleasantly surprised to find that beneath the grayness of an English winter there was a golden thread of active Indian life. The colorful weekends were landmarks to be reached after a dreary week. They went to the temple, a reconverted church hall decorated with Hindi scripts and exhortations and pictures of garlanded pundits. Women sat at the back, admiring each other's saris, giggling and gossiping. Mothers pointed out suitable husbands to their daughters, who either looked coy or became angry. After the last *mantra* was chanted, food was served while the congregation chatted and laughed.

Sunday was cinema day. A local cinema showed films in Hindi and the girls rhapsodized over Shashi Kabur, the latest screen idol. Mai bought Gujarati film books lavishly illustrated with highly colored photographs, and offering products to lighten the skin, darken the eyes, and make the hair shiny. From these they learned of the existence of Wembley Saris, and found out that the Asian Emporium, inserting an advertisement in English, advised that they had "purchased due to unfortunate circumstances exceeding much kohl," which they were "pleasured to offer at sadly reduced prices."

The festival of Diwali came and went. New clothes were bought and gifts of money exchanged. They all went to the temple and to the dances. Girls were chaperoned by their mothers or married sisters to dances that were held once a week. Sumitra and Sandya took their places in the inner ring while the boys formed an outer circle. The musicians sat down on the floor—as the drums began to beat, Sumitra always felt the rhythm obliterating her thoughts. The dancers held sticks, which they clicked as they passed each other. As the pace quickened, as the sitar and tabla chased each other in a wild, controlled frenzy, their feet moved faster, the sticks tapped louder.

An Indian photographer often came to the temple. He specialized in the old style of picture and would wax ecstatic about his skill. "Anyone can draw English photo," he pointed out sarcastically. "Just say cheeses, or watching birdies, mister smile, finish. One day, two days later, mister coming for picture. Picture ready. Picture of mister saying cheeses. No skill, no class." He paused, then continued: "I *study*," and on the word *study* his voice broke and squeaked in emphasis. "I study subject, add sceneries. You saying what you want—flower, clouds, hands—I balance and paint." So the Patels had photographs of themselves taken. Mai and Bap issued magically from the clouds like science-fiction characters. The four sisters appeared to stand in the palm of a gigantic hand. Sumitra had one taken on her own, emanating from the center of a lotus blossom. The photographs were painted with delicate tints, made into cards and sent as greetings and mementos to friends.

Yet they found that, despite these colorful interludes, it was very hard to adjust to their new life. Bap hated his job and could not reconcile himself to the fact that he had no home of his own. He was used to dispensing hospitality, not receiving it. Mai was cowed and ill, and spent most of the time in bed. As the months went by, Sumitra found that she was helping more and more in the home. As soon as she pushed open the door after school, she heard Motiben calling, "Come, girl, you must grind the mustard seed!" or "The house needs cleaning!" or "Iron your father's shirt!"

Because of this, she could not begin her homework until late at night, after she had settled Ela and Bimla in bed. Within ten minutes she was nodding over her books, red-eyed and exhausted. She couldn't concentrate at school and, although she now understood perfectly what the teacher was saying, could not remember a word.

Mr. Jones called her into his study. "We are very pleased with the way you have settled in, and some of your work this term has been very good. But many of your teachers complain that your homework is never complete and that you appear withdrawn in class. Is anything the matter?"

Sumitra studied the carpet. It was duty gray, slightly muddied from the tramping of wet boots. "I'm sorry, Mr. Jones," she said, "I just have to help a lot at home. I don't seem to have much time to study."

"Shall I go and see your parents?" he asked. "After all, I imagine that one of the reasons they came to England was so that you could have a good education."

Sumitra twisted her hair around her finger, making patterns

on the carpet with her shoe at the same time. It was obvious, put like that. But to her family, school was something that finished at 4:30. Her allegiance then was to them. When Hilary went home, it was to a clean house and a hot meal. She did her homework in her bedroom and then went downstairs to watch television. Girls and women in the Indian community were expected to clean and cook. Meals could take up to three hours to prepare. Hilary's mother bought bread from the baker, but *chapatis* and *pooris* had to be freshly prepared for each meal.

She sighed. She felt as if she were a bridge between two countries, two banks that would never meet, two cultures that could never merge. She was like a bridge and everyone was walking over her, from one land to another, like tourists visiting a foreign country but not fully comprehending the strange customs they observed. She pushed her hair back. "Thank you, Mr. Jones, but I will talk to them." She couldn't imagine the kindly headmaster sitting in Leela's house, talking politely to Bap, while Ela played around his feet and Bimla posed her favorite question, "Have you heard of President Amin? I hate him!"

Sumitra tried to explain to Mai that she needed to concentrate more on her schoolwork. Mai sighed. "You must work harder then," she said. "After you have helped Motiben, then you must work."

Nearly two years went by in the same way. They all slowly became accustomed to their changed lives. Then Leela announced that she was pregnant. This news meant that they could not longer remain in the house. Without knowing it, they had unconsciously accepted the Western ideal of a room for each purpose. The house was already overcrowded, and a baby, with all the items it would need, would make life unbearable.

A week before the baby was due, Sumitra was sent off to

the Housing Department. She took Sandya with her, although it meant that they both had to have a day off school. They told the gray-haired housing official that they had been living in the house of a relative for many months. "Our mother is ill and weak, we share a room with our two younger sisters, and our aunt is going to have a baby."

"You realize that there are people who have been on the Council Housing list for years?" inquired the official.

They had never thought about this at all, but looked wise and said, yes, they knew.

"I can only offer you a place in a guesthouse–accommodation where we house homeless families in the borough. That is all I can do, I'm afraid. Will you tell your father, and if he is interested, we'll get someone round to see the circumstances you're living in."

The girls went out into the street. They felt very grown-up and sensible. "I've got some money," Sumitra said. "Let's go and have a coffee."

"Sumitra," protested Sandya, "Bap will be cross!"

"Who is going to tell him?" asked Sumitra impatiently.

Sandya grinned. "O.K."

They went into a coffee bar. The two customers glanced up briefly and then continued munching. The waiter looked up and whistled. The girls pretended not to notice. He came over to the table and wiped it down ostentatiously, leaving behind greasy smear marks and scattering crumbs over their clothes. "Yes, madam?" he asked Sumitra.

"Two hamburgers and chips, and two coffees, please."

"No, Sumitra, that's meat. You know we're not allowed to eat meat. Meat is dirty."

"I eat meat at school, Sandya. It's nice."

"I won't eat it."

"O.K., have a cream cake instead."

Sandya watched fearfully as Sumitra ate her hamburger. She

expected her sister to shrivel up and die horribly. "This is delicious," Sumitra said, squirting on the yellow mustard. Sandya wiped some cream off her chin.

"What is a guesthouse?"

"I don't know, but it can't be any worse than living with Motiben. I get so tired, cooking and cleaning all the time. Even if I had to do it somewhere else, at least there would be four less people to do it for!"

"I bet Bap will refuse to go," commented Sandya. "You know how much he loves Leela."

But, strangely, Bap did not object. He told Sumitra to phone up the housing manager and arrange for someone to come round.

Mrs. Johnson was small and plump. She looked round the house and was shocked. "Six adults and four children living here! I agree that it is intolerable, and will be absolutely impossible when the baby is born. Where do you all sleep?" They showed her the mattresses they arranged nightly in the kitchen, and the chairs and settees they slept on in the lounge. "We can move you to a guesthouse that accommodates homeless families. You would be given two rooms, and breakfast would be provided. There are no cooking facilities, I'm afraid, but the guesthouse is only a ten-minute bus ride away, and I'm sure your relatives will let you come and eat here. When a Council house becomes available in a couple of months' time, we'll move you again."

Sumitra translated this information. No one was enthusiastic. No one was antagonistic. It was just one more move, one more change. The guesthouse was only four miles away from where they were living now. Sandya was due to start at Northfields in September, and Ela would go with Bimla to a new primary school. There was no need for tearful farewells; they would still see Leela and Jayant every day. So they packed up their few belongings and waited to be told when to leave. The night before they went, Sumitra dreamed of fireworks and glass bubbles.

Antonio Moni was Italian. He had dark curly hair and sparkling eyes. He was enjoying the sudden boom in homeless families. Running a guesthouse had been hard, with people always coming and going. He had to smile all the time, even when his bunions were aching. Staff was difficult to find and keep. He was tired. Sheets had to be laundered once a week, food deliveries ordered and checked, and guests got drunk and crockery got broken. He had a wife and three children to keep, and sometimes he lost hundreds of pounds a month in overhead.

When the Council approached him with their proposition, he had discussed it with his wife. The Council had a problem—where to put the hundreds of people who couldn't find anywhere to live. He had a problem—how to fill his empty rooms. The solution was simple and obvious. He could join the growing number of hoteliers in the borough by offering a home to the homeless.

Once Antonio and his wife had agreed to the idea, he moved into action. He went to a carpenter and ordered several pieces of hardboard. A friend in the decorating trade was contacted, and together they partitioned off rooms, putting up false walls, papering the hardboard. "Brilliant!" said Antonio when the work was complete. "Now we can get two families into what was originally one room. I'll have my hotel in Milan yet!" He had already quoted the Social Services Department an exorbitant rent, which they had accepted without a murmur. Of course, Antonio was not thinking of himself. By providing more rooms, he could offer temporary accommodation to more families.

The Council began to send him lodgers. Jean was the first to move in, with her young boy, Francis. She was divorced. Next Rita, an unmarried mother with a baby girl, arrived.

Antonio found them to be no trouble at all; indeed they offered to help when they saw he was overworked, and he gave them a couple of pounds each week in return for their assistance.

Then trouble began. A rowdy family was moved in: a drunken father, a neurotic mother who ran naked about the house in the middle of the night, frightening the ordinary trade away, and two uncontrollable children who disturbed his regular customers, the salesmen and the businessmen down from the North for conferences. One of his most valued visitors, a Belgian doctor who always stayed at the guesthouse when he came to lecture in London, went to another hotel, saying he would never return.

Antonio talked to the family. They swore at him. He phoned the Council. They pacified him. After two more days of anxiety when another salesman cut short his stay, Antonio threatened the Council, saying he would take no more homeless families.

The offending family was immediately removed to another hotel and began the round of bed-and-breakfast accommodations in the borough. Antonio relaxed again. But he had lost two good clients. After this experience, it was a delight to welcome the Patels. The four girls were beautiful and well behaved. The parents were quiet and polite. Mr. and Mrs. Patel accepted their partitioned room without a murmur, they even seemed pleased. A larger room was allocated to the sisters. Ela and Bimla were to sleep in a double bed, and Sumitra and Sandya had a bed each.

To sleep on a bed after months of sleeping on the floor was luxury enough. "Only one rule," Antonio told them. "No cooking. Fire regulations, you understand. And no noise after eleven P.M. There is a television room downstairs which you are welcome to use. Breakfast is served from seven-thirty till nine." He gave them a happy smile, pinched Ela's chin and left them in the girls' room.

Sumitra translated what Antonio had said. Mai was tired. She unwrapped the food she had brought from Leela's house and Sumitra unpacked the plates. They sipped orange juice out of the tooth mugs provided and sat on the beds, looking around them.

"Can we live here, Mai?" Ela begged. "I like it. It's better than Leela's house. We've got sinks in our rooms!"

"Silly girl," laughed Bap. "We *are* going to live here, for a few weeks at least. Then we will get a house. The Council said."

What none of them knew, what none of them suspected, was that the Council said that to every person on their waiting list. They had been saying so for years. The truth was too depressing. It was hard to tell people living in atrocious conditions, with leaking roofs and rat-infested rooms, in overcrowded houses with no inside lavatories, that not enough houses were being built, and that they might have to stay where they were for the rest of their lives. It was easier to say that they would be moved in a few months. This gave misery a time limit, made it finite.

The Patels had no idea that they were privileged because they were officially homeless. They didn't know that English people were living in unsanitary damp houses, just as they had not known the conditions in which the black people in Uganda had lived. It was outside their world, beyond their preoccupation. All they knew was that once they had been rich, now they were poor. Once they had owned a house, now they had nowhere to live. They were homeless—the Council had said—and unbeknown to them, being homeless was the only way to get a house in one year, instead of thirty years.

They were unaware of the system. They had not made it. But they would be blamed for it.

Sumitra washed the plates. She looked for somewhere to drain them. "Sandya, put a cloth on the dressing table," she said. "We'll have to make that into a draining board." They said good-night to Bap and Mai, and went early to bed. They did not sleep. The house was too noisy for that. The television room was directly beneath, and one of the guests seemed to be deaf. They heard, through the floorboards, the *News at 10*, a western movie, the *News at 11*, *The Old Grey Whistle Test*, and then the *Epilogue*.

Footsteps thudded up and down the stairs. Voices called loud good-nights. There were noises on the other side of the partition. Then they fell asleep.

CHAPTER VI

Sumitra soon understood that the clients in the guesthouse fell roughly into two categories: the homeless families and the "ordinary" guests. Ordinary guests were out all day, returning home in the evening to congregate in the lounge with bags of chips and cans of beer. As short-stay customers, they had no need to cook or launder in their rooms.

The homeless, on the other hand, were united in the breaking of Antonio's rules. Printed notices in each room read: 1. NO COOKING 2. NO CLOTHES TO BE HUNG ON RADIATORS. FIRE REGULATIONS. These notices hung alongside the more universal message about vacating the premises by noon on the day of departure. Necessity and infant children forced the homeless to break these commandments. Smelly diapers and wet Babygros could not wait for a weekly visit to the launderette and had to be rinsed out each night and then dried over the radiators.

Some of the families cooked elaborate meals in the privacy of their rooms. Rita had borrowed a Primus stove; Motiben lent Mai an electric ring to boil water for tea. The more adventurous used camping kitchens, and someone even attempted to roast chicken in an enameling kiln. After meals the forbidden equipment was hidden in wardrobes, beneath socks and sweaters or saris, along with tins of food and powdered milk and sugar. The most essential item was the air freshener. When Antonio's car was heard in the car park, the smell of frying sausages was quickly masked by a squirt of Lilac Lady or Lavender Spray and the pan pushed under the bed, to be retrieved with its somewhat dusty contents when the coast was clear. Sometimes Antonio grew concerned that the fire officer might visit and revoke his license, so every now and then he made a spot check. Once he found Rita's electric kettle and confiscated it, with dire warnings about what he would do if any more illegal utensils were discovered. For the following week, the homeless drank orange juice or milk and dined on bread and cheese, but gradually Antonio relaxed his supervision and they began to prepare illicit meals once more.

Jean was the natural leader of this group. For one thing, she had been there the longest and checked and vetted each new arrival, explaining the system to them. For another, her room was at the front of the house, facing the road. From here she could keep watch for new arrivals or prying social workers. When Mrs. Johnson had brought the Patels to the hotel, Jean had peered into the corridor muttering, "Blimey, we're being invaded!" just loud enough for Sumitra to hear. None of Jean's remarks about the "wogs and nig-nogs coming over 'ere and taking our jobs and houses" was ever made directly or loudly enough to challenge. But by her mumbled comments every time one of the sisters appeared in the television room, or as she grabbed her son, Francis, away from Ela's proffered sweets, Jean made it clear that the Patels were unwanted.

One evening Mai sent Sumitra to the shops to buy biscuits. Jean was in the hall, talking to a thin woman with a young baby. She was surrounded by shopping bags full of possessions.

"What's your name?" Jean was asking.

"Maria," the woman replied in a tired voice.

"How long did they say you'd be stopping?"

"A couple of months."

Jean laughed bitterly, and, glancing up, saw Sumitra coming down the stairs. "Sorry, luv, but you're the wrong color. Them nig-nogs'll be out before you and me, you see. I've bin 'ere for five months with no chance of getting out yet!"

She flounced off to show Maria to her room. Sumitra stayed motionless on the steps, her heart thudding with anger. Why was Jean so rude and horrid? Why did she call her nig-nog and wog? Just because Jean was blond and white, she was no better than Sumitra. She remembered Bap's words, "They think they are better than us, just because they are white. But we, we are better than them. They are irreligious, dirty, ignorant people!" Bap was right, these people *were* awful.

"What's up, Sumitra?" asked Martin, the young teacher who lived in the attic, pushing open the front door and seeing her standing by the banisters. "You look like you're about to murder someone!"

"I think I am!" Sumitra tried to smile but instead burst into tears.

"Hey, what's the matter?" he asked gently. "What's going on?"

"I can't stand it. Everyone's so awful to us. They call us Blackie and Paki, and Ela wants to wear tights and long sleeves in the summer so she won't look so brown. I shall go mad! It's not fair!"

She caught Martin's eyes and they both laughed at her unintended pun.

"You're exaggerating a bit, aren't you?" he said. "I'm not awful, am I? Not everyone is prejudiced. You must try to remember that the people here are desperate to be rehoused and fed up of their living conditions. That makes them bitter and cruel. They're only jealous of you because you're young and attractive and have got your life before you. You should be sorry for people like that!"

He clapped her cheerfully on the shoulder and went off to his room. Sumitra sighed as she walked to the shops. Two girls passed, giggling and whispering as they went. They were laughing at her, she was sure, because she was brown. Looking away, she read the KEEP BRITAIN WHITE slogan painted on the side of the post office. She felt lost, threatened. Martin didn't understand. Like most of the teachers she'd met, he seemed to be unaware of the hidden racism that throbbed beneath the surface of daily life. Her sisters were aware of it, her Indian and black friends faced it every morning, evening and night. Little Ela and Bimla were abused by some of the kids at their school, and when they told the teachers, the reply was "Take no notice. It doesn't matter what color you are!" Yet the teachers were never there when these incidents occurred in the playground, when embryonic thugs called her sisters Blackie and punched them and made them cry! Sumitra returned home, feeling savage.

As she let herself in, she heard a baby crying and saw Maria, the new arrival, in the lobby, trying to balance the child in her arms while moving her assortment of packages into her room. "Hello!" She smiled. "Could you give us a hand with these?"

Taken aback, Sumitra helped carry the battered containers down the corridor.

"Thanks, luv!" said Maria. "What's your name?"

Sumitra told her, waiting for the inevitable "Sorry, say it again, slowly." It didn't come.

"Oh, I used to work with a girl called Sumitra. She's gone to America now, but we still write to each other. Will you come and visit me when I've got straight?" She laid the baby on the unmade cot. "This is Sally. Will you come tomorrow?"

"O.K.," replied Sumitra. She ran upstairs with the biscuits, feeling happier than she had done for some days.

Next day after school, Sumitra knocked on Maria's door. "Hi, come in!" Maria greeted her with a huge grin. Sally waved her hands with pleasure and grabbed Sumitra's long hair in a chubby fist. "Sit down!" Sumitra released her hair and looked round for a seat. The room was crammed with furniture, the bed, high chair, seat and cot taking up most of the floor space. Every available centimeter was taken up with baby articles—bottles, spoons, jars, bibs, toys. Sumitra noticed that Rule Number 2 was already being broken. Diapers were drying on a clotheshorse, baby clothes were draped over the radiator. The whole effect was tropical—Maria herself was warm and bright like the sun, and a sweet dank smell, a mixture of baby and air spray, rose from the damp, steaming diapers. "Excuse the mess," apologized Maria, "but it's a bit hard to fit everything in!"

Sumitra removed a pile of clothes from the chair and sat down. "I thought our room was crowded," she said, "but this is terrible!"

Sally pulled at the box of toys under the cot and began to hand them one by one to Sumitra. Maria plugged in the kettle and spooned coffee into tooth mugs. "Well, at least it's keeping us off the streets, and me old man's not here to upset me. How long have you lived here?"

"It must be about a month. We were living with relatives in Highgate before that for nearly two years. But originally we're from Uganda—at least me and my sisters are. Mum and Dad are from India. I was eleven when we left Uganda. I'm nearly fourteen now." She began to tell Maria about life in Africa and the traumas of the last few years. She talked about the difficulties of their last year in Uganda, about the tensions of their long stay with relatives, and about the aggravations caused by people in the guesthouse. Maria listened without interrupting, occasionally questioning or prompting. Sumitra talked on and on. As she poured out her anguish and fury, as she expressed her fears and hopes, one part of her mind was thinking, This woman is listening to me. She's giving me time and space. No one had ever done that before.

"How did *you* end up here?" Sumitra finally asked, realizing that she had been speaking for almost an hour about her own problems. She looked at Maria closely, noticing how thin and gaunt she looked. Maria's black hair contrasted strangely with her pale face; her blue eyes were anxious.

"Me? Oh, it's a familiar story. I married the wrong guy. Dave was working for a wine importer and we got the chance to live in France for a bit, just after Sally was born. Dave started drinking heavily—temptation, I suppose—and things went from bad to worse. A friend got me a ticket to England and I came home with Sally. We've been back three weeks. I didn't have anywhere to live—both my parents are dead and my aunts didn't want to know because they think a woman should stick with her husband through thick and thin—so we've been living with friends, moving from one house to another so as not to outstay our welcome. It's almost impossible to find a room to rent with a baby. Anyway, in desperation I went to the Council yesterday to see if they could help—you know, tell me addresses of rooms to let. They said I was homeless and, as I've got a child, brought me here. They said it was for a couple of months, but according to some of the others, it will be much longer."

"Yeah," Sumitra burst out bitterly, "because of the nig-nogs! I heard what Jean said!"

Sally had been playing with her train set beneath Sumitra's chair. Now she crawled out and tried to clamber onto the girl's lap. Sumitra lifted her up, and Sally reached out for her long black hair with cries of delight.

Maria sighed. "Me dad always used to say that life was tough, so you might as well try and change it to leave something better behind you. Some people call you nig-nog, some people call me whitey. Some people blame you because they can't get houses or jobs, other people blame me. What I'm trying to say is it's the system that's wrong. Name-calling and fighting each other won't change anything. But things have got to change, for your sake and my sake and Sally's sake. I don't want her growing up in a world that is bigoted and vicious. And getting upset over stupid remarks doesn't help. You've got to stand up and show that you've got the same needs and rights as anyone else!"

She stopped talking and scooped up her daughter. Sumitra yelped as some strands of hair remained in Sally's fist. Assuring Maria that she was all right, Sumitra went upstairs, smiling to herself. She had at last found someone to talk to, someone who tried to change things, not be changed by them. So several times a week Sumitra knocked on Maria's door. At last she had found someone to listen to her, a thin, dark-haired woman in a guesthouse for homeless families, thousands of miles away from where she had begun her search.

CHAPTER VII

Although Bap said, "One day, you will see, we will have a place of our own," he didn't really believe it. He sat each night deep in thought before the shrine they had made out of an old cardboard shoebox with pictures of Lord Krishna stuck on with Sellotape and the legend Freeman, Hardy & Willis emblazoned along the top. Cotton-wool candles soaked in *ghee* burned briefly for the *puja* each morning. Had Antonio known, another rule would have been added to the list: 3. NO BURNING OF COTTON-WOOL CANDLES SOAKED IN GHEE. FIRE HAZARD. But the only sign that the Patels were there was the delicate smell of sandalwood joss sticks wafting down the stairs.

Never had life seemed so bleak, so bare, to Bap and Mai. Living in the guesthouse brought them into their first close contact with the corrupt white culture. Everything evil in Western civilization seemed to surround them: unmarried mothers, wives who had left or been deserted by their husbands, families arguing violently. Even the ordinary guests came back drunk late at night, slamming doors, falling up the stairs, swearing loudly, vomiting. Raucous laughter rang out. Bap left the house early each morning to walk wearily to the bus stop, to wait beneath the daubed message PAKIS GO HOME! His life was in ruins—he could not provide his family with a proper home and felt that his work was beneath him. His earning power, his morale, his self-respect were threatened.

Mai stayed in her room all day, too ill and depressed to learn the new language. When Ela and Bimla returned from school, she took them to Leela's house. There she felt safe. She knew what was expected of her, did not have to struggle and strain with each word. The children played with Trupti, Leela's baby. When all the family had arrived back from school and work, they would eat in an island of peace, a haven from which they had to set off each evening, back to the alien ground. Bap and Mai were frightened by the hostility they could sense. So they clung to their own customs, their own traditions. They lived on one side of the hotel and Jean lived on the other, and between them was this great gulf of fear. This fear is concentrated on me, Sumitra thought to herself.

Jean is telling me to go away, and Mai is telling me to stay beside her. Yet I cannot do either. I will have to grow up and live my own life.

"Gooda morning, all right?" asked Josefina, Antonio's wife, as she handed Mai clean sheets each Friday. "Gooda morning, all right?" Mai replied shyly, passing over the soiled bedding for delivery to London Linen, launderers to the hotel trade. This was her only contact with anyone apart from her own family. She waited like the princess in the tower, looking out of the window as people came and went in the alley below. She watched enviously as two friends met, set down laden shopping bags or pushed strollers idly to and fro as they talked. Mai felt trapped. She listened at the door to make sure the corridor was empty before tiptoeing to the bathroom, then peeped out of the bathroom before making the quick dash back to her room. She even stuck a sponge under the tap when she ran a bath, lest anyone complain about the noise of the water, and she bathed quickly, dreading an impatient knock on the door.

Yet even within her sanctuary she felt threatened. The hardboard partition had warped and sometimes the person in the adjoining room would smoke cigarettes. Mai watched in despair as the smoke issued magically out of the wall and clung to her sari. Devout Hindus are forbidden to smoke, so to drown the offending smell she would light a joss stick and watch the blue fumes of the *agar bathi* incense creep vengefully through the crack into the next room in a silent protest, her own holy war.

Mai looked at herself in the mirror. She had lost weight and huge black marks appeared beneath her eyes. She cried. She had never been alone before. Always there had been friends, family, servants around her. She had been part of a large group with its embracing customs and habits and conventions. Indian visitors to her hometown had been immediately welcomed, fed, questioned and accepted into the larger circle. But no one had opened their doors to her in this strange country. She felt the hostility on the faces of the other homeless families, so she closed her door and waited for the day to pass. All over England, Indian ladies waited for the evening behind closed windows, and those who would have smiled at them did not even know that they were there.

Day after day she muttered to herself, "Once I was happy, now I am sad. Once I was strong, now I am weak. Once I was warm, now I am cold." She sang these words to herself like a *mantra*, over and over.

Occasionally on Saturday afternoons, when the lounge was usually deserted, Bap would go down to watch the wrestling on the television. He sat there, absorbed, on the edge of his chair, calling out Gujarati instructions to the wrestlers, imitating the actions of the figures on the screen. Sometimes the girls would persuade Mai to accompany them, and she would sit huddled in the corner. Martin or Maria and Sally might come in and smile at the parents, sit chatting to the girls. But if Jean or Rita popped their heads around the door to see who was there, the girls would hear a muttered comment, "It's too crowded. We'll go in later." It was the same on Sunday mornings when they watched *Nai Zindagi Naya Jeevan*, the program for Asian viewers. As Jean left the breakfast room to get ready to go to church, they could hear her telling Rita, "They've even got their own blinking programs!" She might even come into the lounge to glare uncomprehendingly at the screen and look angrily at the family before flouncing out.

Sumitra was puzzled by the way in which people could transfer their feelings from one to another. Was it telepathy, she wondered, or a residual animal instinct, the instinct that causes a flock of birds to suddenly wheel round in flight? With some people, like Maria and Martin, she felt an immediate warmth. And then there was this cold, evil, silent thing emanating from Jean and Rita, or strangers she saw in the street, although they might not have changed their expression in any way. Sumitra, too, could switch on a range of signals without knowing how she did it. She could generate warmth or cold, love or hate from the top of her head, sending out messages like a spaceman in a science-fiction movie. She steered clear of Jean and Rita because they looked unfriendly, and was attracted to Maria. Jean signaled, "Go away! I am closed in. I don't want to be disturbed." Maria signaled, "Come in and tell me about yourself. Warm your hands at my fire."

Sumitra was puzzled by so many things. "I feel," she confided to Maria, "as if I'm looking for my own identity, something that will tell me who I am. Sometimes it's like walking along a tightrope—just when I've almost reached the end, somebody makes a remark about Indians, or Asians, or immigrants, and I fall off. Do you know what I mean, Maria? Am I Sumitra, a fourteen-year-old girl, or am I just another statistic, a label?"

Though her white school friends seemed to share this same sense of searching, she felt that their conflicts were not so great. Hilary could discuss things with her parents—they helped her with her homework and allowed her a lot of freedom. She could go to discos, stay out till 10:30 at weekends, sleep at friends' houses and go to parties. Sumitra and Sandya were not even allowed to accept invitations to afternoon tea! Mai and Bap would not listen to reason. "No, you can't go! We don't know them. No, they are not Indian. No, discos are dirty! Kissing goes on! Not for us, not for you! *Nati*, *nati*, no, no!" Looking back, she realized it must have been like this in Uganda, too, only there she had been unaware of the social pressures. The colors of the players had changed, but the game was still the same. One had to stay inside the circle. It was all right for Mai, she was content within the ring, but Sumitra could not hibernate in a room for the rest of her life. She sometimes wanted to smash the circle to bits and rush beyond it.

Education was another means to keep her confined. "You must study hard," Mai told her. "That is why we came, to give you girls a good education. You must learn well and pass exams, then you can marry a fine man and be rich, have a good life." Yet Sumitra and Sandya had nowhere to study. The teachers who scrawled *Could do better* and *Try harder* beneath their essays and notes would have been surprised to see the conditions in which the homework had been done. Sometimes they laid their books and pads on the bed, while Ela and Bimla leapfrogged around them and the noise of the television came booming through the floorboards. Once they had tried working in the lounge. Sandya had just spread out her pens on the table and opened her textbook when Jim, one of the other residents, came in, switched on the set and asked if she was doing well at school.

They talked to Bap about it, and he reluctantly agreed that the two older girls could come straight home from school to do their homework, while he, Mai, Ela and Bimla were at Leela's house. In the comparative peace, they were able to work quicker, and would then spend their free time in the lounge. Some of the ordinary guests were friendly and interesting. Dr. Duval, the French embalmist who lectured at University College Hospital, was a quiet, lugubrious man with a white, waxen face. Sandya said that he had probably embalmed himself by mistake. He mournfully helped them with their French homework. Dorothy, or Micro Dot, as she was known, was a large plump machinist, taking a refresher course in design, and was usually to be found in front of the telly, munching packets of peanuts and crisps while bewailing her size. She had offered to make some dresses for Ela and Bimla. Martin was kind and helpful—Sandya soon learned that she had only to complain that she was hungry for him to jump up and go round the corner to Indian Qwik Snacks, returning with steaming containers of curry and cans of Coke, which they consumed sitting on the floor. "No wonder teachers are always asking for pay rises!" Sumitra teased him. "You must spend all your money on feeding the hungry!"

When Sally had fallen asleep, Maria would bring in a pot of tea and they would fetch their tooth mugs. Most nights, Sumitra and Sandya met their friends in the lounge while Bap and Mai, safe in Leela's house, assumed that the girls were studying hard for their marriage certificates, when in fact they were laughing and munching in front of the telly.

Martin had a car. It was neither new nor roadworthy, but it went. When Bap was watching the wrestling one Saturday, Martin asked if he could take the girls out sightseeing some weekends. Punch—Bap's left hand felled an opponent to the ground. "You take them out? All of them? O.K." Martin was after all a teacher, he seemed polite enough and he was clean and tidy. There would be no harm if all the children were together, and if Sumitra went somewhere other than to the temple and Indian dances, she might stop pestering him about discos.

So at weekends the four girls would pile into Martin's car to visit the tourist attractions that they had not yet seen. They watched the soldiers changing guard at Buckingham Palace. They climbed up the Monument, they went down the river to Greenwich. At Christmastime, Maria and Sally joined them to go to Trafalgar Square to look at the tree. A feeling of gaiety was in the air, and people smiled at them—at Sumitra carrying Sally, Maria holding Ela's and Bimla's hands, while Martin chatted to Sandya.

"We should go carol-singing," said Martin, "and collect money for the Save the Children Fund." They greeted this suggestion with enthusiasm. On the way home, they practiced carols, and Martin informed the other guests that night that a choir was being formed.

"Who's going to be in the choir?" Jean asked suspiciously.

"Well, you and Rita, of course—we couldn't do without

you! You'll be the leaders. Then there's Dr. Duval, Micro Dot, and Maria, and Jim."

"Who else?" Jean insisted.

"The Patel girls, and anyone else who's interested."

"Well, I dunno!" Jean demurred.

"Jean, it's Christmas!" Martin said sternly. "Christmas is all about homelessness and helping others."

Jean tried to think of an excuse. "Who's gonna baby-sit?"

"We'll ask some of the other families and guests to help out. It's only for one night!"

"Well, I dunno!" Jean repreated.

"Can I come too, Mum?" begged Francis. "Please let's go!" Her son's eyes began to fill with tears.

"Oh, all right!" she snapped.

The lounge was commandeered for one hour each night while rehearsals took place. "Lanterns, we must have lanterns!" cried Jean, unwillingly entering into the Christmas spirit. "And a tin for collecting the money," Rita added. Martin tapped the table with a spoon. "Come on, let's try 'Hark the Herald Angels.' " Dr. Duval sang a reedy baritone with a nasal French twang; Jim had a vigorous baritone; Ela, Bimla and Francis sang piercing trebles, while Jean, Rita, Sumitra, Micro Dot and Maria wavered between soprano and alto. "That sounds terrible!" Martin complained as they finished the first verse.

"Come off it, mate, we're not *Stars on Sunday!*" Jim told him.

"You're telling me," moaned the choirmaster, making them sing it again.

In the days before Christmas, the house had an air of excitement and purpose, and their singing gradually improved. They decorated the hotel–holly was acquired from the local park and a small tree was dug up from a piece of wasteland. Jean filched Antonio's emergency supply of candles and they stuck them into their tooth mugs. Then on Christmas Eve they set out in the cold, crisp air with their homemade lanterns to beg the goodly householders of the neighborhood for money. Becky, Rita's small daughter, carried the collecting box.

They stopped outside the first house. Ela began to giggle. "Stop that!" scolded Sumitra. Martin raised his hand and hummed a note. "Ready? *Hark the . . .*" The strains of the carol wafted raucously into the sky. The porch light was switched on and a small gray-haired lady stood beaming. "That was lovely, lovely. Please sing another verse." Glowing with pride, the choir continued while the lady joined in. She pushed a coin into the tin. "A Happy Christmas, my dears."

By the time they had been up and down the street, the Save the Children Fund was five pounds seventy-two pence and one Irish penny better off. "One more house," Martin said, "and then we'd better go back. The children will be getting cold if we stay out much longer." There was a block of luxury flats opposite the hotel. "Blow it!" muttered Rita. "They've got one of them posh phone-up things."

"That's all right," Martin said. "I'll push the button to Flat eight and say we're carol-singers. They'll let us in—that must be on the top floor and we can work our way down."

Sumitra grinned at Maria. "Isn't this great? I've never been carol-singing before!"

"We used to go every year when I was little," Maria told her. "This brings back lovely memories. Come on, they've opened the door for us."

They trooped into the lift and pressed the knob for the third floor. Nothing happened. They tried again. The lift slowly edged upward and then stopped with a jolt. The button was pressed again, but the lift didn't move. They were stuck. Martin read out the notice on the door. WARNING: MAXIMUM SIX PEOPLE.

"*Mon Dieu, qu'il fait chaud!*" Dr. Duval remarked helpfully. Sandya watched in astonishment as huge waxy drops began to ooze from his skin. "He really has embalmed himself," she whispered to Sumitra. Becky began to cry. Ela asked, "How much longer will we be here?" Francis said in a plaintive voice, "Mum, can we go 'ome now?"

"All shout together," instructed Martin. "Somebody's bound to hear."

They shouted and screamed till they heard a voice call out, "All right. Don't panic! Keep calm. A fire engine is on the way!"

The choir cheered loudly and then continued to sing carols. Ten minutes later, a siren could be heard wailing in the street below, and soon smiling firemen had forced open the door and were pulling them up the gap between the lift floor and the landing.

The residents of the flats were waiting as they were hauled to safety, and Becky's tin was soon filled up by sympathetic contributors. They sang "Once in Royal David's City" with everyone, including the firemen, joining in, and then they ran down the stairs into the cold night air. "I can't wait to tell the others that the fire engines came to rescue us," said Maria. "They must have heard the sirens from across the road." The choir ran across the street, laughing and shouting. They held hands in a rush of friendship as they ran up the hostel steps. Jean and Sumitra and Rita and Sandya held hands on Christmas Eve.

CHAPTER VIII

A newcomer moved into the room that had been previously occupied by Dr. Duval. Passing along the corridor one day after breakfast, Sumitra saw the door open and called out, "*Bonjour, Monsieur, il fait beau aujourd'hui.*"

"*Bonjour, Mademoiselle,*" replied a friendly voice in an atrocious French accent. "Please, were eez ze room for ze, ow you say, breakfast?"

Sumitra saw that the dark-haired, waxen-faced Frenchman had turned into a lanky young Englishman. She grinned, showing him to the dining room. "Sorry, I thought you were someone else. Here you are. I've got to dash now!"

"See you later," called the stranger.

First lesson was Russian. They were studying Pushkin's *Poema Lyubvi—Love Poem.* Mr. Cherny was trying to fire his pupils with an appreciation of the subtle nuances of the language, and seemed unaware of the whispering and scuffling in the back two rows. "*Ya vac lyubil; lyubov yeshjyo, boot-moszhyet.* George, translate this line for us."

George began, falteringly, "I loved you." The class wolf-whistled and clapped derisively. Mr. Cherny smiled with pleasure, his voice grew deep with passion as he continued: "Love still perhaps has not *entirely* perished in my heart. *Sovcyem*—entirely. By the use of this word, the poet indicates that his feeling is not yet dead."

Sumitra glanced at her watch. There were another thirty-seven minutes to go before Maths. She amused herself by drawing thirty-seven short lines on her book, by which time two minutes had elapsed and she marked off a couple of strokes. Thirty-five more to cross out.

Love—*lyubov—l'amour—prem—chavoon.* Sumitra listed the words and began to color them in, wondering as she did so what love was, what it felt like to be in love.

Her thoughts drifted back to the guesthouse and to the young man she had met that morning. The hotel was like a frontier town, a staging post, where people came and went in swift succession. A room that one day had housed a large businessman down from the North, would open the next to reveal a petite woman on a shopping expedition from the Highlands. The sex, shape, color and occupation of the residents changed mysteriously from week to week.

She had liked the look of the newcomer, and she liked the way he had looked at her. He was one of the warm people, like Martin and Maria. "I loved you silently, hopelessly," declaimed Mr. Cherny. "*Byezmolvno, byeznadyozhno,*" clasping his hands to his heart and looking into the distance in some remembered ecstasy. The back rows guffawed and cheered. Sumitra checked the time and crossed off another nineteen strokes. Sixteen more to go. It was no use her speculating about the new man. Even if she got to know him and they liked each other, Bap would never let a friendship develop. Romantic love did not feature in their life. Bap had married Mai without ever having met her or seen her first. Sumitra felt like A. C. Pushkin, condemned to love *byezmolvno, byeznadyozhno,* silently, hopelessly. . . . Even casual friendships with male school friends were taboo.

Before Sumitra went into the lounge that night, she brushed her hair and changed out of her uniform. Martin was sitting watching the news. Sumitra was disappointed—perhaps the new arrival had only stayed for one night. She pretended to watch telly, then looked up as the door opened, and the stranger came in. "Hello," said Martin. "What's your name?" They soon found out that he was called Mike, was twenty-one, came from Bristol and had been working as an assistant manager at a shop called Hanbury's in Bath. He had just been transferred to the Finchley branch.

As Mike spoke to Martin, he looked at Sumitra, seeing a slim girl with beautiful, almond-shaped brown eyes. "I'm going to get Maria," Sumitra announced, feeling suddenly embarrassed. When she had left the room, Mike asked, "Does she live here alone?"

Martin smiled sympathetically. "No, there are three younger sisters, and the parents. They've got two rooms upstairs."

"What a beautiful girl," Mike sighed.

When Sumitra came back with Maria, they all began to talk casually about jobs and the difficulty of finding accommodations. Rita and Jean came in to watch the play. They chatted to Maria, glancing occasionally at Mike, sizing him up. Strangers in the frontier land were always a threat or a promise. Jean and Rita subtly included Mike in their conversation, inviting him to join in, while at the same time Sumitra sensed that they were trying to warn her off, without Mike noticing. She also saw that Mike kept glancing at her, and that Jean and Rita were giving each other annoyed looks.

Sandya rushed in. "I can't do my Maths. It's really hard. I never understand algebra—it's rubbish! What do I want to know algebra for!"

"I think I still can remember my algebra," said Mike. "Bring it in and I'll have a look."

Sandya dashed out, pigtails flying, and they heard footsteps thudding up the stairs. Jean and Rita were looking even more cross than ever.

While Sandya was upstairs, Mike asked if they knew anyone who would be interested in a Saturday job. "We've got a vacancy for a clerk, mainly keeping stock records and adding up loads of figures. There's a calculator in case the clerk runs out of fingers."

"I could do with a Saturday job," Sumitra told him eagerly, "but I'd have to ask my father first. He might not agree."

"Well, I could take you and bring you home," Mike suggested. "It would all be useful work experience."

She'd been half-thinking about Saturday work for some time. It was hard for Bap to keep all of them on his wages. He had to find dinner money, pay for uniforms, give them fare money and buy food and clothes. He could have claimed for free meals and a uniform grant, but no one had told him about these benefits, and even had he known, he would not have wished to be identified with the feckless English poor. So he struggled on, trying to make ends meet, with a sick wife and four growing girls. If Sumitra took a job, at least Bap would not have to worry about her, and she would be able to buy some smart clothes so that she would look like her friends at school, even if she didn't feel like them.

"I think he'll agree," Sumitra said. "I think I'll be able to persuade him. When could I start?"

Jean stood up suddenly. "Come along, Rita!" she ordered.

Rita gave a start and obeyed. They both sniffed in unison and walked out of the room. Sumitra could hear them in the corridor saying, "Typical. Wogs taking our jobs!"

When she heard her parents come in, Sumitra followed them to their room. "Bap, would you mind if I took a Saturday job? There's someone who's moved in, he's a manager, the manager of Hanbury's in Finchley. He's a friend of Martin's, and he said he'll give me a lift there and back. Come down and meet him, *please,* Bap."

Unwillingly, Bap went to the lounge with his daughter and was introduced to Mike. Mike told him about the job, explaining that Sumitra would learn about office procedures and would earn three pounds each Saturday to begin with. When Bap realized that no traveling on public transport would be involved and that Sumitra would be gaining useful experience, he shrugged. All the children of his friends were taking Saturday jobs. What could he say? He felt diminished in this strange land and, besides, even three extra pounds would help his limited budget. Perhaps, too, it would be good for the girl to start learning office work—it would be harder for her to eventually get a job than for a white person—and as Mike was a friend of Martin's . . .

"Go, go, it's O.K."

Mike smiled and Bap turned to Sumitra, saying in Gujarati, "Any trouble and I won't let you go anywhere, understand?"

Sumitra was overjoyed. "Thanks, Bap. Of course there will be no trouble. Why should there be?"

Working on Saturdays at Hanbury's seemed to establish Sumitra as a person in her own right. Often she had felt that she was merely a representative of her family, or of Asians, or of immigrants. Too often she had heard muttered words, "All their fault—buying up our shops—taking our houses." Sumitra would feel mortified and humiliated. She wanted to scream, to shout that it was not true. But it seemed to be true, if exaggerated. Newspaper shops and sub-post offices were being bought and managed by Asians. How could she deny this? Every time an immigrant family was rehoused, it meant an English family had to wait longer for their turn.

There was not much time to think or worry at Hanbury's. Here she was simply Sue, the Saturday girl. Her job was to deal with customer inquiries, answer letters and do the books, not to sort out the country's housing problems or racial issues. The first morning was very confusing, but after Mike had shown her round, Pat, a bustling, gray-haired lady, took over and explained the work. Pat sat with Sumitra all day, ready to help and advise. At 11:00, she asked Sue to make the coffee, and when it was ready, Pat helped her carry it round and introduced her to the other members of the staff. To her relief, they all seemed very friendly.

"Come on, dear," Pat said at midday. "Let's go and have

lunch." She took Sumitra to the sandwich bar across the road and chatted amiably about her daughters, her husband, her grandchild. She brought out pictures of the family and showed them to Sumitra, pointing out items of interest. Sumitra relaxed. I wonder how old she thinks I am? she thought. Pat was treating her like a friend instead of an inexperienced teen-ager. It was like that for the rest of the day; she was a workmate, a colleague, part of a team, paid to do a job. Getting three crisp pound notes in a brown wage envelope like Bap's as she left was an added bonus. She would not have minded working for nothing!

This Saturday job became a lifeline to Sumitra. It gave her a measure of security and was sometimes the one solid thing in her week. Because her function there was laid down, described, bounded, no one threatened her and she threatened no one. When the February half-term came around, Mike asked if she could work for that week. Bap agreed and Sumitra received six days' pay. She gave half her wages to Bap and bought presents for her mother and sisters with the rest. At Eastertime she worked during the three-week school holiday. She began to feel that she really belonged. When Mike's director gave her an Easter bonus and an Easter egg, wrapped in silver paper and decorated with a blue satin ribbon, she was thrilled. "I'll never be able to thank you enough for getting me this job, Mike!" she told him as they drove home that evening.

With the money she had earned, Sumitra was able to buy some new clothes. She went shopping with Sandya and bought suits for them both. Discovering that she had a good dress sense, she found it was possible to look elegant on very little money. They went to Wood Green and Finchley market, coming back with bags crammed with bargains. Sumitra twirled round in Maria's room, showing off her new skirt and heels. "You look beautiful, Sumitra!" Maria exclaimed. "Mind you, you even look lovely in your school uniform, and that's quite an achievement!"

Maria was always telling her that she was beautiful. But Sumitra wasn't sure if that could be true. Ela and Bimla didn't think that brown skin could be beautiful. They teased each other, taunting, "You drink too much tea." "You shouldn't eat so much chocolate! That's why you're so brown!" Yet one of the guests, an artist, had asked if he could paint her portrait. He had left the unfinished watercolor with her, showing a girl with deep bronze skin, huge, glowing eyes and a sensitive mouth, looking bravely from the page. Did she really look like that, or was it an artist's prettified impression? She knew it was wrong to worry about looks. After all, everyone said it wasn't what you looked like that counted, but what you were. But that didn't seem to be true. The prettiest girls, the handsomest boys, found life easier at school, as if their pleasant features attracted popularity and praise.

Throughout the year, Martin had continued to take the sisters out at weekends; now Mike sometimes joined them. He became fascinated by Indian history and religion and started to learn Hindi. He made a point of being up in time to watch *Nai Zindagi Naya Jeevan* with Bap and Mai on Sunday mornings and asked questions about the language. Bap was pleased by Mike's interest.

One day it began to snow. Mai's coat was still at the cleaners. Sumitra asked Martin to collect it for her. On wintry nights he would give Mai and Bap lifts to Leela's house. The parents were grateful. They wanted to thank these people who were helping them and their children. They had to admit that Martin, Mike and Maria were different from other white people, if only because they were white people they knew, instead of white people they didn't know.

So when Gopal's marriage was arranged, they invited their

friends to the ceremony. Sumitra was to be an attendant and left early in the morning to help dress the bride and paint the complicated patterns on her face and hands. The others crammed into Martin's car and Mike's van and set off for the hall in the afternoon sun. Sandya was detailed to explain the proceedings.

Gopal and his bride were sitting on the stage, the guru chanting in front of them. Guests filed past, paying their respects and laying gifts on the floor. "You see the shrine, that's where people make offerings of food to the gods." Sally heard the word *food*, saw where Sandya was pointing, and was off, up the side steps, past the astonished guru and the beflowered bride and groom. Happily, the little girl began tucking into the food of the gods. Nuts, sweets, candies were consumed before Sumitra, positioned behind the bride, realized what was going on and hurriedly caught her up. Sally was passed along from hand to hand, back to Maria. All the guests, the guru, the bride and groom began to laugh. Sally buried her head in Maria's neck and sobbed. One of the women hastily brought a plate of *jalebi* and offered it to the child. Sally gave a damp smile and began to eat.

We all laughed, thought Sumitra, *yet really this wedding is no laughing matter.* It underlined her own fast-approaching future. An arranged marriage, a life spent cooking *chapatis* and *pooris* and rearing children—she shook her head fearfully. But what else could she do? Without consciously realizing it, she had been concerned about her future for years.

She felt very confused. She could not say whether this confusion arose because she was an Indian in England, or a woman in a man's world. It was easy to blame disappointments on the fact that she was brown—many of her friends did this. But during her stay in the guesthouse, she had met white people who had lived hard lives—lives certainly harder than her own had been in Uganda.

Maria had told her stories about the slum street in which

she had lived as a child, where the neighbors would call in to borrow sugar or tea on a Thursday night, and how everyone would disappear when the lookout boy came racing down the street to say that Old Fred the rent man was coming. Maria knew all about pawnshops and scrag ends, and stuffing paper in shoes to keep out the cold.

Maria had left school, worked in boring jobs, married, had a child, and now was living in a tiny room at Antonio's, living in fear lest the landlord discover that she had an electric ring and a kettle. Maria couldn't blame her life on the color of her skin. Sumitra smiled, glancing down into the hall where her friend stood, Sally in her arms, talking happily to a group of women in gorgeous saris. Maria wasn't the sort to blame anyone. She would just say, "Well, that's the way it happened, and it might be for the best, who knows?"

Jean and Rita, however, blamed their misfortunes on the color of their skin. Sumitra had heard them in the lounge, saying, "If I was black, I'd have got rehoused by now!" "If I was colored, they'd have given me that job!" And Indians blamed the fact that they were brown for not getting jobs and houses. Was this, she wondered, a device to cover up inadequacy? In order to preserve the myth of difference, people had to line up in rows of black, or brown, or white, and hurl their inadequacies like bombs at each other. That way they would never meet, never discover that really they were the same.

The guru chanted on. Guests continued filing past; the stage was now laden with gifts and offerings. Of one thing Sumitra was certain: She would never agree to an arranged marriage. She wasn't even sure if she would marry at all. But just for today, she wore a sari and smiled and sprinkled rose water on the bride and groom and joked and laughed.

CHAPTER IX

Once a fortnight, Bap told Sumitra to phone up the Housing Department. "Tell them to move us! Tell them we need a place of our own!" He had overheard the other homeless families on the public phone in the hall, telling the Housing Department that they needed a place of their own. This seemed to be the only way of reminding officialdom that they were still alive.

"Nine months I've bin 'ere!" Jean complained to Rita at breakfast one day. "Nine bleeding months! And there's immigrants I hear of getting rehoused in only two weeks. It ain't fair!"

The four Patel sisters were just finishing their toast. "Hurry up, Ela," said Sandya, glaring at Jean. "We'll all be late for school!"

"I really hate Jean," Sandya seethed as they waited for their bus. "She always says such nasty things."

"They are nasty," agreed Sumitra, "but sometimes what she says is true! Look at the Choudris and the Shahs. They've only been on the housing list for two months and they've been rehoused already. Jean says she's had her name down for years, and she's still waiting. She blames us for it, although we don't allocate the houses. It all seems crazy to me—it *is* unfair."

A bus came into sight. "Can you see what number it is?" Sandya squinted. "It's a twenty-six." They shouldered their bags and squeezed onto the platform. Sandya was pushed to the back; Sumitra grabbed a seat rail and stood swaying as the bus jolted along. Perhaps, she thought, some homeless immigrants got rehoused quickly because they had exotic reasons for not living in hotels. All Maria and Jean and Rita could tell their social workers was that they couldn't stand it any longer.

Their children had nowhere to play. They could not be fed properly. They had to be kept quiet so as not to annoy the other guests, yet were disturbed by the drunken clamor and constant activity. These were stock complaints, the clichés of homelessness.

She knew that Mai's friend, Mrs. Shah, had told her social worker that she was not allowed to pray in the same room as a menstruating daughter. This disrupted her religious life, she said, so the family was rehoused. Another family, the Choudris, had complained of the difficulties of preparing food according to Hindu custom, and had been quickly moved to a maisonette. At the temple, they had met a family who had been living in bed-and-breakfast accommodations for six weeks. Their elderly grandmother had risen at five o'clock to greet the dawn by singing the Usha *mantra* very loudly. This may have pleased Agni, Lord of Fire, but unfortunately the neighboring guests were unappreciative of such devotion. The family was hastily rehoused on an estate built with reinforced concrete walls.

Mrs. Johnson had explained to Sumitra that the Council operated a points system. This seemed to be a game like bagatelle in which marks were scored and added. Everything that counted as a misfortune was given five points. Children counted as a misfortune, so if someone had five kids, they gained twenty-five points. Religious difficulties equaled five points. A serious illness or mental disability scored five more marks. When a family reached the jackpot they got rehoused.

Sumitra realized, along with the other homeless, that the only way to work the system was to nag. The more things you could find to complain about, the better. So everyone pretended that their children were ill (5 points), that the head of the household was on the verge of a breakdown (5 points), that their sons and daughters could not study in such conditions (5 points). The trouble was that everyone was saying the same kind of thing so the scores were canceled out. Return to Square One. Some realized that the only way to be rehoused was to have another baby (5 points), but this would only add to the housing problem in twenty years' time!

Sumitra had been phoning the Council for months. "I'm calling on behalf of my father, Mr. Patel, at Antonio's Guesthouse. We've been homeless for so long. We aren't allowed to cook and we can't get the food we're used to, and my sister and I can't do our homework. My mother is ill—she has a doctor's certificate to say that she should be rehoused. Please, can you help us? We're getting desperate!"

These regular calls produced two visits from Mrs. Johnson, who assured them that their case would soon be coming up for review. Then the harassed social worker would rush off to see three other families to whom she would offer the same hopes. The phone calls and the visits had become like an act of worship, a *puja*, now mechanically performed and barely believed in.

The bus stopped with a jolt. Schoolchildren pushed off, laughing and shouting as they made their way to school. The day continued as usual. In assembly, Jonesy talked about the poor inheriting the earth. The history lesson dealt with the British Constitution and democratic government. In the playground, National Front leaflets and Trotskyist pamphlets were passed round, and a fight broke out between supporters of the rival groups. After school, a young man waited outside the gates recruiting for the British movement. Sumitra and Sandya hurried home to make the phone call to the Housing Department.

This time, the lady who told them that their case was being reviewed at the next meeting happened to be telling the truth. A letter arrived from the Council the following week. Bap brought it into the breakfast room for Sumitra to translate. Jean saw the buff envelope and left the room looking bitter. Sumitra ran upstairs to tell Mai. They had been given a temporary furnished flat in Hendon. Mai turned to the wall and wept. Sumitra put her arms round her mother, and Sandya and the two little girls clambered on Mai's bed, bouncing up and down with excitement. They could hardly believe it. A home, after so long, a place of their own.

The news spread like wildfire from room to room. The warmth and friendship generated by the Christmas spirit disappeared. Jean and Rita made a series of angry phone calls to their social workers. The sisters stood in the upper corridor, hiding behind the banisters, and heard them. "Them bloody nig-nogs. I've bin 'ere for over a year. They've only bin 'ere for a few months. It ain't fair. Me dad fought in the war, and I'm stuck in 'ere with me kid. I've paid taxes for years and now them bleeding foreigners . . ."

"I think it serves her right, don't you, Bimla?" Ela whispered. "She's so horrible!"

Maria came upstairs to congratulate her friends, and Martin arranged to take them to see the flat that night. It was in a pleasant, quiet avenue, the top floor of a converted cottage. They piled his car high with goods, and then crammed in, around and on top of their belongings. The flat was roomy, with a small kitchen, two large bedrooms, a box room, a lounge and, to the children's delight, a long garden.

Packing cases were collected from Leela's garage. Articles that had been in storage were unwrapped from the tea chests and marveled over as if they were new. There were items that they had long forgotten. "Look!" shrieked Ela. "Here is my Teddy. Leela gave it to me. I'm too big for it now. I'll let Trupti have it." She danced about, falling over chests and boxes, till Bap shouted and told her to go and help.

Bap unwrapped the shrine. He had made it from wood and carved the Hindi inscription himself. The wood had been cut from a tree in their Ugandan garden. He placed it carefully on the bricked-up fireplace and, seeing it standing in the Victorian house, Sumitra was suddenly reminded of the squat and solid chair she had noticed all those years ago in Mr. Sanghvi's shop. The chair had seemed incongruous and out of place amid all the profusion. Now the shrine seemed strange in the stolid English room. Its curls and flourishes came from another world.

Sumitra stayed home from school on the day of the move. Maria helped her to pack their few remaining articles. "I can't believe we're really going," Sumitra told her, sitting back on her heels and stringing up a box. "I'm a bit frightened. I can't imagine us being a family again."

"You'll be all right." Maria looked at her friend and smiled. Sumitra was becoming ever more beautiful. Her long black hair shone; her eyes, troubled now, were large and dark; and her brown skin glowed. "You are a strong person, you know—you'll survive—and, anyway, you know where I live! I'm not likely to get rehoused for a while. You can come round to see me whenever you like." Mai brought in some saris and shirts from the other room. "I'll miss you all," Maria remarked. "I'm glad you've got somewhere, but I feel like you're my own family."

Sumitra translated Maria's words. Seeing Maria's sad face, Mai said haltingly, "You coming my house all days."

As Mai and Sumitra cooked the meal that night in their new kitchen, Martin and Mike helped Bap move the furniture around. Maria and Sandya tidied the bedrooms and started weeding the garden. This was overgrown like a jungle, and Bimla, Ela and Sally played hide-and-seek behind the nettles, running and screaming with delight till Mai shouted from the upper window that they mustn't disturb the neighbors.

They were served a feast of *pooris,* vegetable curry and potato soup, followed by *gulab jamun* and *jalebi.* Martin, Mike and Bap were served first, with Bap commanding his wife and daughters to fetch another plate, some more water.

The guests had brought housewarming presents. Mike had

ordered some colorful Indian prints from an Oxfam catalog; Bimla found some Blu-Tack, and they stuck them on the walls after long discussions about the best position for each one. Martin's gift was a brass footballer won at a school raffle. This was immediately placed in the shrine, where it joined the ranks of divinities. Maria gave Mai a basket filled with sweets and nuts. Sally disappeared down the stairs and into the back garden. They heard her toiling up again, panting heavily, and she toddled into the room proudly bearing a muddy stone. "Present for Mai," she announced. They all laughed and clapped. The stone was washed and laid next to the footballer, while Mai cuddled the child on her lap.

As she waited on her father, Sumitra realized that he was changing back into his old self. He was being assertive, even bossy. He told his wife and daughters what to do, where to put things. He was scolding and complaining. This sudden change of character was even more startling because of his self-abnegation of the past few months. It was as if his personality had been drowned in the no-man's-land of the guesthouse. Now he was marking out his territory. This was his house, and here he reigned. He was an Indian father, once more head of an Indian family.

There had been times in the hotel when he had longed to reproach his daughters, but there, they had the advantage. They knew the language and had begun to copy the customs of the country, talking familiarly to other guests, cheeking the men. He had been unable to argue or reason with them when they could bring the force of the alien culture to bear on his own deeply held views. He could not shout or insist when a raised voice would be heard and commented upon by hostile residents. Now he was once again master in his own house. His daughters would conform to his society, dress as he wished, behave as he required. Life had always been like that, and now it was as if the short intermission, unbearably long as it had seemed at times, had never been.

Sumitra looked at Mai. Mai was exhausted but happy. The black lines were still there under her eyes, but the strain had gone from her face. She was now mistress where before she had been unwanted guest. Sumitra felt a premonition of foreboding and went to sit by Maria. "I'll miss you, Maria. I'll miss our chats. Can you come round every weekend? Please."

"Of course I will," answered her friend. "By the way, I've just thought. I'll go and ask your mum if she'd like me to come and help her get straight tomorrow." Maria went into the kitchen to speak to Mai. Mai smiled and shrugged her shoulders. "*Su che? Mane kabar porti nati!*" she said. "No understand." Poor woman, thought Maria in a rush of sympathy, she has been living in England for years and probably hasn't understood half of what's been going on around her. Sumitra had followed her into the kitchen. "Can you translate, Sumitra, and tell your mum I can teach her English when she's settled down. In fact, I ought to have thought of that before. I could have taught her at the guesthouse. Still, better late than never!"

Mike and Martin came through. "Sally's almost asleep, we better be going." They thanked Mai for the meal, and Maria turned to her. "I'll see you tomorrow—I'll see you all soon. Don't forget to come round." At the bottom of the stairs, she turned back to wave good-bye. Six pairs of wide brown eyes peered over the banisters. As she closed the front door, she could hear Bap barking out orders.

Ela and Bimla were settled into their beds. They shrieked and giggled till they fell asleep. Sumitra and Sandya were sent to wash up the dishes, while the parents unpacked cases in the sitting room. "I'm glad Mai and Bap are happy," Sumitra mused. "But I'm so sad! We had it good at the guesthouse. I know it was hard living on top of each other and we got fed up with all the noise and people like Jean and Rita, but at least we were free to mix and talk with the other guests." Sandya looked at her and saw a tear on her sister's cheek. She put her arm round Sumitra and then began to cry herself. Drops splashed into the washing-up bowl.

"If only we'd stayed in Uganda," Sumitra continued, "or if only we'd lived on our own all the time. But we've seen what freedom is, and now . . ." Her voice faltered and stopped.

"At school," Sandya commented miserably, "we've been reading the story of Moses. He was allowed a glimpse of the promised land, but he couldn't enter it. That's what happened to us. I'm going to miss Martin and the others so much, I can't bear it."

They were now back in a world of prescribed formalities. The conventions demanded that they obey their parents unquestioningly, were partners in arranged marriages within the Patel clan, carrying on these traditions so that their own children would be preserved in the same mold. Sumitra fell asleep at last in her strange bed, dreaming of eternal incarnations. She saw herself locked in a *samsara*, a cycle of life and death in which she was condemned forever to perform the same futile gestures and from which she could never escape; continuing for ever and ever Om and Amen, because no one would ever break the chain.

In her dream she saw Kali, goddess of war, waiting outside the school gates. The four-armed deity held Rita's dripping head in one hand, Jean's in the second, while with the third and fourth she distributed National Front and Trotskyist literature. There were queues jostling to join the parties, and, with a start of horror, Sumitra saw Bap enlist for the National Front, while Mai waited to sign with the Trotskyists. Mai clenched her fist in a rebel's salute as Bap shouted, "Pakis go home!" Sumitra screamed as she was born again and again and again. She screamed with each reincarnation, but nobody heard.

CHAPTER X

Another Sunday afternoon. Mai and Sumitra were preparing food for the evening meal and cooking batches of *ladoo* and *balushai* for use as snacks during the week. Bimla and Sandya had gone with Bap to see some friends. Ela was playing hopscotch with Emma, who lived next door.

Sumitra took a stick of sweet butter and watched as it slithered and melted in the heavy pan. Adding the farina, she heated it gently, then mixed in the sugar, almonds and cardamom. Rolling the mixture into small balls, she left them to harden.

I wish *I* could harden, she thought. Then I wouldn't feel things so much. She sighed, remembering the conversation she had had with Martin and Maria last night.

"Thinking is uncomfortable," Martin had said. "It's much easier to be a sheep than to be a lone wolf. Sheep just follow the leader and say, 'baa.' But if you're not a sheep, you have to think about things and weigh them up for yourself. The trouble is that there's no such thing as TRUTH. But authority can't accept that. In order to obey, you must accept. So if you're a born thinker, you're a threat, even if you can't help it."

It was strange, looking at Martin, to hear him talk like that. He always reminded Sumitra of a sleepy hippie, with his knees almost sticking through his faded blue cords, his trouser legs finishing suddenly to reveal three inches of delicately turned sock. But she had listened eagerly to what he had to say. He was one of the few people who ever talked to her as if she were an adult.

"Then of course," he went on, "most people don't have time to think. They accept the view of their families, or their school, then marry someone else who agrees with them and carry on the business of working, living and teaching their own children the principles which they themselves have accepted unthinkingly."

"But you're a teacher," she reminded him. "How can you teach if you don't agree with passing things on?"

Martin had tweaked her ear. "You're getting too clever, young lady," he said. "If I were a rich man, I wouldn't work at all. But I have to earn my living somehow, and the teaching profession needs brilliant thinkers like me. I try to free my pupils from their parents' mistakes, not force them into a mold."

"Bashful, isn't he?" Maria remarked. They laughed. But Sumitra had agreed with what he said.

The front door banged, bringing her out of her reverie. Ela came running up the stairs. "Yes, Mai," she said. "What do you want?"

Mai looked up in surprise from the *dal* she was stirring. "I don't want you, Ela. Go back and play."

"But a lady said you wanted me!"

"What do you mean?" Sumitra asked her, puzzled. "What lady? What did she say?"

"You know, the lady with the fat legs from Number seventeen. She said why didn't I go back home. So I came to see what you wanted. Didn't you want me?" Ela stood balancing on one leg, her black hair hanging untidily round her face.

Sumitra and her mother exchanged glances. "The lady must have made a mistake," Sumitra told her sister. "Go back and play."

Ela snatched two biscuits off the plate and ran happily out of the house. Mai and Sumitra looked out of the window at the two children munching the biscuits and chalking fresh numbers on the pavement.

"Someone said that to me when I was waiting for a bus the other day," Mai said softly. "A man, quite young, about twenty-six or twenty-seven. I was just standing in the queue, and he said loudly to his friends that he wished all foreigners would go home. Now people are telling Ela the same. Why do people say these things? How can they be so cruel to a child? Why do they hate us?" She gave the *dal* an angry stir.

Sumitra looked at her mother. "There are always silly people who say silly things. Just ignore them. Think of the English friends we have. They would never speak like that."

"No, but that's different. English people in general are horrible. Sometimes I hate them. Remember those women at the guesthouse, the way they looked at us, the way they treated us. Sometimes they made me feel unclean. And look at the television. Every night someone is mugged or raped or murdered. The English are a savage and rude nation. These things would never happen in India. There, people care about each other."

Leave to harden. Sumitra wished that she could grow a hard shell to encase the passion and confusion inside. "I don't think that's true, Mai," she argued. "People die of starvation in India and nobody cares. Not every English person mugs and rapes. Only the worst things are shown on the news. Anyway, you chose to come to England. We could have gone to India, couldn't we?"

Mai pulled her sari more closely around her and clucked her tongue. Her voice became sharp with irritation. "I've told you before, we came to give you all a good education, so that you can marry well! In India we could not have afforded to educate you properly. We would not have had anywhere to live. If anyone had got ill, we could not have paid for a doctor. It's not easy with four children!"

Why did you have four children, then? Sumitra thought. With servants and houseboys, of course, having sixteen children or one child was the same thing. And if they had come to England for its welfare state alone, no wonder people were telling them to go home, wherever that was! Once more she felt like a bridge, belonging nowhere, seeing both sides of the problem. This capacity to observe dispassionately was making her life so difficult. If only she could have been more partisan, like her mother, and seen things so definitely. Mai was so sure that she was right. After all, they harmed no one; they lived in their house, went their own ways, kept within their circle of friends.

Mai smoothed the hair from her forehead. "Sometimes I think we *have* made a mistake. Maybe we should have gone to India. At least there we would have been among our own people."

Sumitra was silent. She couldn't really talk to her mother. To agree would be dishonest. To disagree would provoke a scene ending with Mai in tears accusing Sumitra, Sandya, everyone of misunderstanding her, of not appreciating the sacrifices she had made. After all, it was for their benefit they had come. Mai would much rather be living in India.

Sumitra knew Mai was unhappy and tired. She had found a job in a shoe factory in Enfield, which employed Asian women at inferior rates. She left home each morning at 7:30 and arrived home in the evening after the long bus ride. There were the girls to attend to and her husband to pacify. Weekends were a busy rush of cooking, cleaning, temple-going, visiting or entertaining. And there was always this other thing to contend with, the fear, the hostility, the knowledge of which lay somewhere in the back of the head, pressing down coldly, debilitating.

Mai went to lie down. Sumitra took her a cup of tea, tidied up the kitchen and went into the lounge. Switching on the telly, she curled up on the shabby sofa, pushing her finger in and out of a hole in the cover. She watched the screen and tried not to think.

Since they had moved, Sumitra had felt isolated. At the hostel she had a community of friends; in Hendon she knew no one. Her schoolmates lived in Finchley or Highgate, so there was nobody to whose house she could walk when she felt like talking. And Bap wouldn't let her travel alone at night. It was so difficult to explain to her friends at school why she had to go straight home after lessons. She saw her schoolmates talking in gangs and was reluctant to withdraw from the ring of companionship. But someone had to be home to look after Ela and Bimla.

She was not allowed, either, to go to discos or parties. These, according to Bap, were common, dirty pursuits. The only knowledge he had of English life was what he read in the more dramatic newspapers and, like his wife, what he saw on the news. He felt like the Defender of his Faith, a bastion against Drugs, Sex and Drink. He loved his daughters and did not want to see them abused and exploited by the vile culture that seemed to surround them. So he kept them, by the force of his personality and the power of his traditions, within the magic circle of his control. No one was to go out alone at night, no one was to go to English clubs, no one was to attend teen-age parties.

"What do you want?" he asked, trying to understand. "We go to see friends, we go to Nagin's house, we go to the cinema, we go to the temple. Don't you like the dances at the temple? What do you want with discos? That's not dancing, anyone can do it!" He pranced around the room, giving his interpretation of Pan's People from *Top of the Pops*. Sumitra and Sandya laughed unwillingly. Ela and Bimla clapped their hands and joined in. "You see, you see," he encouraged them. "We go out a lot. We go to Leicester and to Wolverton and to Milton Keynes. What do you want with discos?"

They did go to Leicester and Wolverton and Milton Keynes. That was true. But all they saw of these towns was the inside of somebody else's kitchen.

The only concession Bap now made was to allow them all, occasionally, to visit their school friends at the weekends.

They could also bring their friends home whenever they wished. This in itself was a victory.

When Sumitra invited Hilary and Lynne to tea, they were delighted. They arrived in their best dresses and were fascinated by Ela and Bimla. Bimla greeted them with her usual question, "Have you heard of President Amin? I hate him!" but she spoke the words now without much conviction. It had simply become second nature to her, almost a conventional icebreaker. "Isn't she sweet?" gushed Lynne. "And isn't Ela adorable?" Sumitra introduced her parents, who smiled shyly and muttered a few words of welcome. Mai went out to make the tea, and Sumitra and Hilary followed to help.

Lynne began to tell Bap about school. He nodded his head intelligently, occasionally interjecting, "Fine, fine," or "Not, not," when it seemed to fit. Lynne was enthralled. He had such a cute accent. As Sumitra brought in some *rasgullas*, Bap turned to her in anguish and asked, "What is she talking about? I can't understand what she's saying." Lynne thought he was telling Sumitra what a pretty friend she had. She felt flattered.

"Can Sumitra come to the dance next week?" she asked him. Sumitra grimaced behind Bap's back. She knew he wouldn't let her go. Lynne winked at her. She could get anything out of her own father by sitting on his knee and rubbing her fingers across the back of his neck. "It's a school dance, on Wednesday." She smiled. "Please let her come, Mr. Patel. My mum will drive her home. *Please.*"

Bap got up and left the room. "He won't let me go," said Sumitra. "It's no use asking."

The next weekend, Sumitra went to Hilary's house. "Be back by six," Bap told her.

Mrs. Patterson had left plates of sandwiches and scones on the kitchen table and poured out the tea from an enormous china teapot. Sumitra was surprised to find the house was shabby and the furniture old. Somehow she had always imagined that Hilary's home would be luxurious. Mr. Patterson was a tailor, tall and stooping, with horn-rimmed glasses slipping off the end of his nose. Hilary's mother was small and fat, with three aprons tied around her middle. "I wear them to keep myself clean," she explained mysteriously. Hilary shrugged her shoulders and grinned.

"Come and see my room," she said. Pictures of Steve McQueen and Abba decorated the walls; the bookcases were full of useful texts, and an old desk stood in the corner. They peeped into Greg's room. Greg was a prefect at their school—his room was like a study, with shelves of paper and pens and biological specimens lying around. A microscope stood on the cupboard.

The house was old, but the atmosphere was one of warmth and trust. Hilary and Greg were treated as equals, working in the same direction as their parents, not as servants and inferior beings.

Lynne's house was completely different. Her father was a company director, her mother an elegant and sophisticated ex-actress who now devoted her spare time to good works and charitable organizations. Lynne had a portable telly in her room, thick pile carpet, and a divan covered with shiny red satin drapes. They ate tiny sandwiches off bone-china plates, so thin that Sumitra could see her fingers through the bottom. A Shetland pony was stabled in the back garden.

Now that she had seen some of her classmates' homes, she found it even harder to reconcile the life she led with the lives she saw her English friends leading. Her days were made up of school, homework, housework. She had to look after her sisters, and by ten at night her brain was so tired that all she could do was sit down and gaze at the screen. She had formed the impression that all her fellow pupils went home to a cooked meal, a clean house, a smiling mother who helped her child off with her coat, poured tea, cleared a space for the student and brought in drinks and snacks to the busy worker. This rosy picture was a composite of what she knew of Hilary's mother and an ad for drinking-chocolate. The discrepancy between her own life and this image made her bitter and angry.

She knew her parents wanted her to succeed, but she didn't see how this was possible when so many demands were made on her. It was different for Sandya. Sandya seemed to be more traditional, less questioning. But then Sandya was only twelve. Perhaps she would react more strongly when she realized what sort of life she would have to lead. And the little ones, Ela and Bimla. They seemed happy enough at the moment. They enjoyed school and looked forward also to the festivals and celebrations at home and at the temple. But when they grew into young women, what would happen then?

These questions seemed to have no answer. They were like the question of why people were different colors. There seemed to be no reason at all, or if there was, Sumitra was no nearer to finding it now than she had been as a child. She knew the anthropological answer now, of course. People had evolved in different regions, different climates, so their pigmentation depended on the degree of sunlight it had to bear. But what puzzled her was why one color thought they were better than another. And now, when successive migrations had brought people of one color to live with people of another color, why didn't they just assimilate and forget about the shade of their skin?

Once she had been in the park with Martin and Maria. She watched the dogs playing with each other. An Alsatian had raced across the grass to sniff a little poodle, then a spaniel had joined in, until seven or eight dogs, all different colors and breeds, were rolling and playing on the field. They had been united by their dogness. But people were not united by their humanity.

The figures flickered across the television screen in front of her. Other people's tragedies and fantasies made her own seem less immediate. She saw life stretching bleakly before her. Had she never come to England, the problem would not have existed. She would have grown up in an Indian community and learned to perpetuate its culture. But now she was being educated in one way, surrounded by boys and girls who appeared to be free to choose their friends, their careers, their future partners, to make what they could of their lives, while she was restricted. She was daily allowed a glimpse of the promised land, had even lived in it for a while, but could no longer enjoy its advantages.

Last night Maria had said to her, "Not all English people are as free as you think. We have the freedom to choose, but often our choices are limited by our chances. Look at me!" She laughed. "Look what I have done with my freedom. I'm twenty-six years old, with a two-year-old baby, and I'm living in a tiny, smelly room in Antonio's guesthouse. Sometimes I envy Indian women. Their husbands have been chosen for them, they know what their lives will entail, they seem calm and happy. I'm not saying that I'd want to live like that myself; I don't think I could stand it, but then they probably wouldn't want to live like me. All I'm saying is that Jean and Rita and me were free to choose our own husbands, and we all made bad choices. Some Englishwomen choose well, and are happy. Some Indian women are happy. But no one is really free. We all are restricted by our families, or our culture, or our particular century."

"Shut up!" Martin had told her. "You sound like a philosopher!"

"Did you hear that, Sumitra?" Maria had laughed. "He told us to think and now he's trying to stop me!"

Sumitra sighed again. On the television, a cowboy was bleeding to death. She rose and fetched a hairbrush, then returned to the sofa, brushing her hair with long strokes. She knew she needed time to think. Perhaps it was good that her life had been turned upside down; otherwise she might have been one of the nonthinkers. She stared at the screen again. A woman was performing miracles with a packet of soap powder. One moment the clothes were black, the next they were white. White, bright, pure, shiny. White is clean. Black is dirty. Black is beautiful. A child is black, a child is white. . . .

It was easier to watch television than to think. It was like that at school. She could hear the words the teachers were saying, but couldn't find the meaning behind them. She felt as though something were sitting on her head, as if she wore a label on her like a leper. She was brown in a white world, restricted in a free society, old in a young body. Nothing she could do was right. So she watched telly at home, and at school sat calmly at her desk while her mind left her body and went to secret playgrounds in the sun.

Whenever her work was done, she watched television. It was her household god, comforting, informing, soothing, entertaining. It was her personal guru, which she could turn on or off at will. It seemed to her that in a way she was part of the mass culture churned out each night. There were slots for certain programs—westerns, dramas, news, comedies, documentaries. It was possible to predict what any particular program would present. Almost every program was a repetition of the formula necessary for its type. And she felt as if her life, like the life of the heroines on the screen, were a repeat performance prescribed long before her birth.

At school they were reading *Macbeth.* She had been gripped by Macbeth's vision of Banquo's sons, line after line of kings reaching to eternity. She had been reminded of Talika, her childhood friend, whose life had been predestined. Talika had been a reluctant bride but now, living in Birmingham with her husband and five children, had seemed passive and almost content when last seen at Salah's wedding. Line after line of dutiful Indian wives stretched out before and after her. Sumitra knew that her place was somewhere in this line.

So she watched television. Even when Maria and Martin and Sally came round to see her, she watched television. It was safe and warm inside the set.

CHAPTER XI

One by one, the families in the guesthouse were rehoused. First Jean, then Rita, received the long-awaited buff envelope from the Housing Department. Eventually Maria, having sadly watched all her friends leaving, was offered a flat.

All the Patels were invited to the housewarming party; and to Sumitra's surprise, both Mai and Bap agreed to go. She realized with a shock that, although they had now been living in England for years, this was the first time that they had all been asked to an English house.

Maria had attempted to cook an Indian banquet. "I've felt awful not being able to offer you anything more than tea or coffee," she said, "so this is to make up for it." Unfortunately, the only items of furniture she possessed were a camping stove that Martin had lent her, a three-legged chair from a rubbish heap, and the trunk with which she had traveled to France and back.

Maria had prepared a huge pan of rice with peanuts and tomatoes. She brought it into the dining room and put it on a sheet on the floor. "I'm sorry there aren't any chairs," she apologized, handing round an assortment of cracked plates. Bap laughed. "In India, no chairs!" and they sat down gracefully, cross-legged, helping themselves from the pan and quickly professing that they were full up. "It tastes a bit funny," said Ela. "Did you burn it?"

"I did burn it," Maria admitted, "but I thought you might not notice. I put in some more cardamom and butter sticks to hide the taste." She went to make some coffee and came back with a tray of cups and biscuits. Mai and Bap smiled as if it were the most natural and pleasant thing in the world to eat burnt offerings at housewarming parties in empty, uncurtained rooms. Sally plumped herself on Mai's lap, pulled at her nose, touched her caste mark and chattered away in her unintelligible language.

There was a ring at the door. Martin came in carrying bags of *samosas* and coconut cakes. Ela and Bimla fell on these hungrily. "I've got a bed on top of the car," he told them. "Can you help me bring it in?" he asked Bap. The two men heaved the bed into the hall. "Someone at school said they had a spare bed and I've just been round to pick it up."

"That's great." Maria grinned happily. "I was beginning to wonder if Sally and me would be sleeping in the trunk tonight!"

"I like your flat," said Sumitra. "It's really nice."

"Well, you can come round whenever you like; you can come and stay when I've got another bed. You are all welcome, you know that."

As Sumitra helped wash up, Maria said to her, "I mean it, you know. Anytime you want to come over, whether it's to see me or to just get away from things, or just to sit and think, come."

Sumitra shook her head. "Thanks, Maria, I know you mean it, but I'm so busy at home, Mai would never let me. She'll let me visit, but she'd never let me stay."

Every now and again, when he had been particularly upset by an incident at work, Bap would say, "Things will be different when we get our shop." This was what he and Mai dreamed of, a little shop with overhead accommodations, like the one Jayant had just bought. At the moment, this was part of the family folklore, the same as the longing of English urban dwellers for a little cottage by the sea. It was a dream, a myth, sustaining them through long bus journeys and dreary days, a dream which they knew might never come true but which enabled them to carry on. Bap and Mai would say, "When we get our shop," as Mr. and Mrs. Jones said, "When we get our cottage." Meanwhile they were living in temporary Council accommodations and subject to the whims of the Housing Department.

They had grown to love their home in Hendon. It was warm and cozy, and the garden was full of the vegetables and roses they had planted. There were two Indian grocer shops in the main street and this made shopping easy. They had settled in so well that they had all forgotten it was only a temporary address. So when Mrs. Johnson turned up one day with a rosy smile and news of a larger house, they were all surprised and taken aback.

"Fortis Green! Where it is?"

"Fortis Green! How will we get there?"

"Fortis Green! No, we staying here!"

Mrs. Johnson was patient but adamant. "I'm sorry, I realize it must be unsettling for you, but we need this flat for other people. The house in Fortis Green is much larger and you'll have it completely to yourselves. The Council has a lease on it for two years, and then we will be able to provide permanent accommodation for you. As for the traveling, it's just as central as Hendon. It's quite near East Finchley tube station. Go and see it. There are four bedrooms, a sitting room and a huge garden. The children will need more space now they are all growing up."

"We must move again!" Bap complained. "For two years,

and then? How much longer will this continue? All the time we were in Uganda, we lived in one house, twenty years in one house. I am not used to changing about. It is not healthy!"

Mai was upset, too. "How can we buy carpets when we don't know what size rooms we will have eventually?" She wanted a house with carpets and decent furniture, color television and a washing machine, like everyone else. She was no different from the average British consumer, though the comparison would have shocked her. "We are lucky to have anywhere to live," Bap told her, suddenly becoming fatalistic. "We must be grateful."

They went to see their new home. Mai walked straight-backed in her sari, tightly holding Ela's hand. "Mai," Ela objected, "you're hurting me!" Mai continued to pull the child along as if she had heard nothing; Bap and the other girls followed behind. She walked as if locked into herself. She hated these moves, having to meet new neighbors, never knowing if they would be friendly or hostile. Each minor rebuff, each new meeting was an agony. So she walked tall and straight and isolated, and, behind net curtains, faces looked out and said, "Look at her, who does she think she is!"

"Here it is, Number twenty," said Bap, opening the gate. Ela and Bimla scampered up to the top floor; the parents and Sumitra and Sandya explored downstairs. There was an enormous room leading out into the garden in which late summer roses still bloomed. The large kitchen led out to a dining room from which the flowers at the back could be seen. They had to admit it was lovely.

Once again, Martin and Maria helped them to move. This house was unfurnished, but Maria had been given a lot of furniture she did not need. She provided three rickety chairs and two sagging mattresses. Bap bought a cooker and the Welfare Department gave them an assortment of divans and an ancient sofa. This sofa became a family joke. Springs stuck out of the wadding and, if they were pressed, they played tunes. The musical sofa made different sounds according to who was sitting on it. When Bap got up, it made a low, resonant noise; for Mai, a higher-pitched groan; and for the girls, a correspondingly thinner note was emitted according to their weight. The sofa was soon covered with an old sari and placed on a ragged piece of matting.

"I'm really worried about my sister," Sandya said to Maria one day. "Fortis Green is so far from anywhere. We'll be really isolated at the weekends—we'll be stuck out in the wilds with no friends."

Maria didn't need to ask which sister Sandya meant. "I wouldn't call this the end of civilization!" she replied. "I'll still come and see you like I used to. You won't get rid of Sally and me that easily!"

"I know, but since we moved from the guesthouse, Sumitra's really changed. There, she was always laughing and chatting. Now all she does is watch the telly. I think she's going mad. She doesn't hear when I talk to her. She just sits and stares at the screen, but when you ask her if the program is good, she says, 'What program?' "

Sumitra felt that she was going mad, too. In the street she felt Indian, at home she felt English. Nowhere, nowhere did she feel like Sumitra. But who was Sumitra, and what should she feel like? Maria had noticed her friend changing, withdrawing from the real world like a nun into a convent. Maria felt a strength, a purity within the girl, as if she were somehow apart, able to fight the world, but lacking the means at the moment to do so.

Mai took Sumitra to see the *hakim.* The *hakim* was an Indian doctor practicing two methods of medicine—he could offer either standard British prescriptions or traditional Eastern cures. "English or Indian?" he asked. Mai hesitated a moment. "We'll try both," he suggested, "to be on the safe side." He examined Sumitra thoroughly and diagnosed anemia. They came out of his surgery with a prescription for iron tablets and a small bottle of syrup labeled in Hindi.

Dutifully, Sumitra finished the bottle of iron tablets and the syrup. But she still felt tired. "I just want to sleep," she complained.

They took her to the temple—there she was lulled by the songs, by the chants; she wore a sari and felt safe. But outside in the road, she felt threatened and weary. "I wish you'd talk English in the street!" she said to her mother. "I don't like talking Gujarati in public."

Mai was puzzled. "I only speak Gujarati," she replied.

A pundit came to the temple to speak to the congregation. He exhorted the children to cling to their culture, to learn the language of their parents. They could all speak some Hindi and Gujarati, but few could write the scripts. A few eager worshipers, led by Jayant, organized evening classes on Wednesday nights. Sumitra was thankful that she was able to write and read these Indian alphabets. But Sandya, complaining that she had too much homework already, was made to go to the first class. An enthusiastic Jayant collected her. He felt that this was one way of preserving the purity of the culture, of ensuring that the Indian community keep together. He was suspicious of his relatives' friendship with Maria and Martin, but although he had tried to influence his brother-in-law, Bap had been adamant. Maria and Martin were good friends, Bap had said, and he would not hear a word said against them.

When Sandya came back, she refused to go again. The teacher was too slow and she already knew the alphabet. All she needed, so she said, was practice in reading. They compromised. Motiben was going to India soon and they asked her to return with Hindi and Gujarati primers. Motiben undertook this commission, but, in the excitement of meeting old friends and relatives again, forgot about her promise until the last day of her visit. She dispatched a servant to go to the bazaar and buy the books, and when he returned with the primers wrapped in white paper, she hurriedly stuffed them into her case and left to catch the plane.

"I hope Motiben forgets those books," Sandya said to Sumitra. "I've got so much work to do already without learning to read Gujarati."

"I know what you mean," Sumitra sympathized. "That's what I feel like. There's always an essay or notes to be written up, and with all the visitors we get, I seem to do nothing but cook. It all seems so pointless."

She resented visitors. They took her away from the television and made it necessary to prepare more *chapaṭis*, more *samosas*. And the guests always seemed to talk about the same things. "Life in Uganda was so good. Do you remember, Charulatah, how the sun always shone? Do you remember Diwali in Kampala?" But Sumitra remembered other things, too. She remembered how some of the Indian ladies had spoken about their African servants, calling them dirty, stupid, lazy. Now in England, they themselves had labels stuck on them. They were supposed to be greedy and acquisitive, though they were no more so than any other group. Sumitra remembered Cooky. She had not been stupid. She couldn't read or write, but she was full of homely wisdom and stories and love. Why shouldn't her children have a chance to be educated and run their country?

"It's really unfair," Sandya complained, "the way girls always have to do the cooking. I wish the men would help sometimes!"

"It's the same at school," Sumitra told her. "When I asked Mr. Rogers if I could join the car-maintenance course, he just laughed and said that girls weren't encouraged to take those lessons. I was so surprised I didn't know what to say. We're supposed to have equal opportunities at school, but it's not true. At least at home no one pretends we're equal. We're not. We're all Bap's servants!"

"Doesn't it make you sick, though," Sandya cried. "I can't bear it when visitors come and all the women scuttle into the kitchen to help make the meal and the men just sit in the lounge and chat." It was true, the women served the men first, and then they ate in another room.

"Yes, but Maria said that when she was little, her dad used to go off to the pub while her mum stayed at home and did the housework. She reckons that things haven't changed very much; that only the laws have changed." In this, at least, Indian society seemed better. There was no pretense that men and women had equal rights. There was no deception, there were no false laws.

It was strange that it was only recently they had begun to question the workings of power. Everyone seemed happy with the arrangement. Women guests would bustle around helping to make *samosas* identical to the ones they had prepared the night before and would prepare the next day. It made no difference to them where they prepared them. It was a woman's duty to make *samosas*. To Sumitra and Sandya, however, it seemed incredibly unfair.

Martin and Maria came round one evening to offer them an old cupboard they had found in a junk shop. Martin took the cupboard into the lounge while Maria stuck her head round the kitchen door.

Mai and Sumitra, both already tired from work and school, were mixing flour and oil for *chapatis* and stirring yogurt into *samosa* dough. Piles of mustard seed lay in the bowl, waiting to be pounded. Their faces were hot and sweaty; their clothes and hair reeked of hot fat.

"It's O.K., don't worry, we haven't come to stay," Maria hastily reassured her friends. "We've just brought you round a cupboard." She looked at the scene, hesitated, and then spoke to Mai. "Mrs. Patel, you know I love Indian food, but you must admit it takes a long time to make. So I'm going to let you into a secret." Sumitra translated this while Maria paused dramatically. Then she lowered her voice and continued: "There's a special sort of food they sell in English shops. It's long and round and you cut it into slices and spread it with butter and jam. It's not too expensive and it takes about two minutes to prepare. You should try it sometime!"

Mai smiled. "Bread, no!"

Maria nodded. "Bread, yes! Indian food is great if you've got a lot of time or a lot of helpers, but you haven't. You should be sitting down now and resting, and Sumitra should be doing her homework. Why don't you eat English food on weekdays and Indian food at the weekends? You can cook lots of things without meat and eggs, and you wouldn't be so tired all the time."

"Mr. Patel," said Mai. "Mr. Patel he no like."

Sumitra went to look at the cupboard and say hello to Martin and Sally. As they went to the door, Maria told her, "If your dad helped, that would be fine, but he doesn't. He's tired after work, so he must understand that your mum is, too. And you've got your homework to do. It's not fair."

"It's not fair," Sumitra agreed, "but it's more peaceful if we do it this way. I can't stand arguing all the time. I never seem to stop arguing, but all I want is a bit of peace."

Motiben brought round Sandya's book. Sandya thanked her sadly, and slowly opened the package. "I hope it's all right," said Motiben, "but Ganesh's servant bought it for me and I haven't had time to check it."

Sandya grinned with delight and relief. She held the book out triumphantly. It was called *Learn Urdu in One Week* by Y.L.A. Kabir, M.A. (URD), Ph.D. (SANS) (ENG.).

"Let's see," said Sumitra. Flicking over the pages, she began to read out the English translation. At the back of the book were stories in Urdu script on one side of the page and in English on the other. "I can't believe that Y.L.A. Kabir is really an M.A. and a Ph.D.! Listen!" The unfamiliar English related a tale about a toad and a snake who were quarreling over a piece of bread. A dog, who just happened to be passing by, advised the pair to "take half-half. An eagle was flying above. It was too hungry. It seized the disputing toad and snake in the nails and flowed away. The peace was being left upon the ground."

The peace was being left on the ground. It seemed so little to ask for, Sumitra thought, a little peace, a little space to be. But at school she was being pressed to make decisions about options for O-levels. She wanted to be an air hostess, had wanted this from the day of their flight from Uganda. She held the memory of the kind hostess on the plane as an icon before her. She wanted to travel to different places, to help confused and bewildered people. But her reports from school were bad. Her teachers told her she was not applying herself to her lessons. She wondered how well they would apply themselves, if they were helping to run homes.

Mai and Bap did not know what she did at school; her teachers did not know what she did at home. It was as though she had three personalities: the workmate at Hanbury's, the schoolgirl, and the daughter. Her parents never went to parents' evenings, did not want to become involved. Besides, they couldn't talk English, they said. They could by now, of course, cope with most situations, but it was a good excuse, one used by hundreds of people. "I don't understand English" was another way of saying "I don't want to know about that." So Sumitra plaited the three threads of her life, like the Rakhi at Rakshabandhan, trying to make them one, while each strand made its own demand upon her. School, work, home—another identity, another ethic, another personality.

CHAPTER XII

Two important events brightened the gloom. Martin and Maria got married and Bap bought a washing machine.

One Saturday, Mai took Sumitra and Sandya to Wembley Saris. The Bengali salesman was suave and ingratiating. Beads of perspiration decorated his upper lip and his whole face gleamed with salesmanship. "Come, maharajin," he said to Mai, taking her by the arm and leading her to the counter. "Yellow cloth, very fine." Sandya suppressed a giggle. He saw her smile and misinterpreted it as a mark of approval. "And for the small one, purple or red." He held up a length of chiffon bordered with gold. Sumitra ran her fingers through some green and blue silks. The man pulled out roll after roll of gaily colored cloth. "See," he said, jabbing at the edging, "border of golden peacocks. He will look lovely, lovely." They chose four rolls and waited while they were wrapped up.

They arrived home with arms aching from carrying their purchases. Ela and Bimla tore open the wrapping. "Mai, can you make us saris, too?" "Please can I have a long dress like Bapti's? Please, Mai!" The evening was spent measuring, cutting, and hemming with the old sewing machine stuttering away. Bap produced some soap that he rubbed vigorously on the needle. The machine still stammered and the new cloth was marked with soap. "No matter, it will smell nice and clean," Bap said happily, watching his family spreading bright colors on the carpet and the girls trying to fasten the saris. "No, no, like this," he demonstrated, taking the purple cloth from Ela and wrapping it deftly round his trouserband. He tucked the lengths neatly through his belt and threw the last yard triumphantly over his shoulder. "See," he said. Mai roared with laughter. "You look like Motiben!"

There was a ring at the bell. Bap tore off the cloth, adjusted his trousers and helped them to clear up the mess. Ela was sent to peep through the letter box. "It's only Maria and Martin," she shouted loudly. "Open the door," said Mai.

The visitors came in, looking shy and embarrassed. They stood together, whispering, "You tell them," "No, you!" until Sumitra asked, "What's the matter? Stop dithering about and say whatever you want to!"

Sally climbed onto Bap's knee and took a deep breath. "My mummy's getting married and Martin's going to be my daddy and you are all coming to the wedding."

Everyone crowded round the couple, congratulating them and smiling. "About time, too," Sumitra said. "I wondered how much longer you'd take to decide. When's it going to be?"

"Next month. You will all come, won't you?"

Maria looked so radiant that Sumitra felt a pang of envy. Would she ever be happy herself? Martin was watching Sally play with Ela and Bimla. Then he turned to Sumitra and said, "I've been clearing out my room as I'll be moving in with Maria. I've found my old guitar. Would you like it?"

"Yes, please!" Sumitra had wanted a guitar for months. Hilary was learning at school and had taught Sumitra a few chords, but Sumitra needed an instrument to practice on.

Martin brought the guitar round the following Sunday. It was enormous and had a strange jangly tone. He showed her a few notes and Sumitra soon picked them up. She disappeared into the kitchen for a few moments and then returned. "Listen to this," she said, strumming some chords. "Guess what it is?"

" 'Angie Baby.' 'Baa Baa Black Sheep.' 'Rivers of Babylon,' " they suggested, looking at her face to see if they were right.

"Idiots!" she said crossly. "Can't you hear it's 'Greensleeves'?"

"Let me have a go." Bimla pulled the guitar out of her hands.

"Sumitra, come and help!" Mai called.

When she had brought in the tray of tea and cakes, Sumitra picked up the guitar again. It made a strident, elephantine noise. "Bimla," she accused, "you've twisted the keys, haven't you?"

Martin took the guitar. Just as he was tightening the top string, it gave a sickening twang and snapped.

"I'll get another string and put it on for you next time," he promised.

Sumitra sighed. She really wanted to learn the guitar, and now she actually had one, but she wouldn't get much time to practice. And even if she did, a five-string guitar wasn't much use. Somehow the whole of her life became concentrated in the E string of the old guitar.

When Maria restrung it, Sumitra thought to herself, If the string doesn't snap it means I'll pass my O-levels. Maria tuned the upper string, and, just as Sumitra had known it would, it broke again. "It's all your fault, Bimla," Sumitra said bitterly. "If you could only leave my things alone, it wouldn't have happened!"

"There must be something wrong with the guitar," Maria said. "That's why Martin gave it away."

"What a cheek!" protested Martin. "It was perfectly all right for years. There must be something wrong with Sumitra."

Sumitra took the guitar to school. The music teacher fetched an E string, tuned it to the correct pitch, and it snapped. "That's strange," he mused. "I wonder why that's happened. You'd better practice on five strings for the moment."

There were now two weeks left before the wedding, and one

week before Sumitra's O-levels began. The guitar was put on top of a wardrobe and forgotten.

"I wish I'd worked harder!" wailed Lynne as they sat in the refectory. "Dad'll be furious if I fail."

"My mum's going to buy me a coat if I pass," Hilary said.

"My father said I'll have to leave school if I don't," Mark told them.

Sumitra didn't think her parents even realized that these exams were any more important than any other end-of-term test. She had tried to explain, but they had just nodded and gone on looking at washing-machine catalogs.

They were all laden with good-luck symbols. Hilary had some heather in her handkerchief, and Sumitra had a tiny elephant charm given to her by Leela. Lynne wore an ivory cross blessed by the pope, and one of the boys had his father's lucky pen.

They queued outside the hall like condemned men. "I've forgotten all my French," Peter said worriedly, opening his textbook and muttering, "*Je suis, tu es, il est.*" The hall looked unfamiliar. Desks and chairs were arranged in long straight lines with a numbered card on each place. Miss Watkins and Mr. Jones were having a last-minute conference, and Mr. Baxter, the Maths teacher, was putting out the question papers. The welfare assistant brought in a tray of glasses and a water jug.

"Go and sit down at the desk bearing your candidate number," Miss Watkins called in an unnaturally high voice. Sumitra wanted to giggle. It was like a farce; she knew all these faces, this place, but everything had changed. "Write your names on the front of the answer book," commanded the teacher. She looked at the clock; it was almost 9:30. "You have three hours in which to complete the paper. You may begin."

Sumitra looked at the translation. Did *pomme de pin* mean pineapple or fir cone? She had never seen the word before. Was *le garçon* wandering through a tropical plantation or a northern forest? Reading on, she found the word *neige* so guessed *pomme de pin* meant fir cone. She finished the translation and turned to the essay.

Running her eye over the list of titles, she chose *Les Vacances* as being the least difficult, and wrote a simple fantasy about a holiday with *maman et papa* in Leicester. Struggling to fill up the page, she felt a sudden wave of hatred as John put up his hand for another answer book. She was conscious of Miss Watkins walking up and down the rows, her clumpy shoes banging out an irritating rhythm on the parquet floor. Then Mr. Jones came in and spoke to the teacher in a loud whisper for about ten minutes. Sumitra wondered what they were talking about. Was it something urgent, had the wrong papers been given out, or was he asking what she'd like for dinner!

After the exam, they filed out, giggling with relief and comparing notes. "What's *pomme de pin*?" "I think it means pineapple." "No, it can't, it said Jean was in the snow!" "No, that was a trick phrase, he was eating tinned pineapple in the snow."

"I know I've failed!" Anne said dramatically, but as she always got over seventy percent in French, no one took her seriously.

"You did all right. You asked for more paper," Sumitra reproached John.

"No," he protested. "I wrote a load of rubbish. I've got big writing anyway. And *you* looked quite happy."

"You must be joking! I couldn't remember a thing."

So they carried on, some convinced that they had failed, hoping against hope that the examiner would pass them anyway, and others convinced that they had passed, but needing the safety net of assumed failure to protect them from possible disappointment and mockery later on.

The week passed by—Russian, Maths, English, Science, Home Economics. Before each one was the same thrill of anticipation, afterward the same protestations of amnesia. By Friday night, Sumitra felt tired and irritable. She went home and soaked in a hot bath. Maria was getting married the next day.

The girls wore new dresses and saris for the wedding. Maria had on a deep green skirt and top, and Sally was in a simple white frock. Martin looked almost smart in his old gray cardigan and new blue trousers. Some children from his school were waiting outside the Registry Office, pockets bulging with bags of confetti. Sumitra recognized Jean and Francis, Rita and Becky among the guests. Mike was there, too, with a pretty blond girl. Martin's family was in full attendance, and Bill, one of his younger cousins, chatted to her after the ceremony. "Come to the reception in our car," he said. Bap started to look annoyed. Sumitra shook her head. "I better not. I'll see you there."

Maria's flat was brightly decorated with paper chains and lanterns. There was fruit juice for nondrinkers and plenty of beer and wine for everyone else. Jean drained her fifth glass of whiskey. "Here's wishing you luck, love," she said, and the guests raised their glasses. She made her way over to where Mai and Bap were standing in a corner and put her arm over Bap's shoulder. "We used to live together, didn't we?" she said loudly. "Give us a kiss for old times' sake." She planted a kiss on his head, nodded apologetically to Mai, and swayed over to where Bill was exchanging addresses with Sumitra.

Bap was shocked. "Come, come on, we must go now! We have to go!" He collected his children and thanked Maria and Martin. "You see what English people are like!" Bap said as they made their way down the hill. "Not Martin and Maria, of course. They are different, but that woman, *she kissed me!* This is not how decent people behave. I will not have you girls making friends with white boys. I forbid it!"

Sumitra folded the paper with Bill's address on it and winked at Sandya.

They were going to Nagin's house. Nagin, it turned out, knew a man whose brother had an uncle whose son worked at a wholesale warehouse. He could get washing machines at a discount. The warehouse was in Hemel Hempstead. They piled into Nagin's car and went to look at washing machines. The uncle's son, Kirit, looked appreciatively at Sumitra as the party went in, and meaningfully at Mai. Mai noted the glances and decided to speak to Nagin later.

They looked at washing machines. One had an extra-large porthole, another a three-compartment detergent dispenser. There were machines with five programs, or ten programs. Sumitra suddenly remembered how Cooky had washed their clothes in the river, beating out the dirt on the rocks.

Kirit advised, questioned, demonstrated. "Six of you. That's a lot. May I suggest the large-capacity machine with a programmed selector dial." Mai nodded. "We can deliver on Monday," he promised. Mai smiled happily. There was so much washing to be done and Sumitra didn't always have time to do it. The children needed clean shirts every other day for school, and their socks got so muddy. She herself did not have the strength to wash clothes by hand, and she was frightened to go to the launderette on her own. A washing machine would be like having a houseboy.

On Monday, Mai took the day off work to supervise the installation of the machine. "Where is it?" yelled Ela and Bimla, dashing in from school that afternoon. "Where have they put it?"

"It didn't come," Mai said sadly.

"Honestly!" said Sandya in exasperation when she heard the

news. "You and Bap make me so cross sometimes. Why couldn't you go to a shop in the High Street and buy a machine there? Just because Nagin knows someone who knows someone, why did you have to buy it from them?"

"They are Indian," Mai replied. "They will not cheat us. We help them, they help us. We are foreigners here. We must stick together."

"That's nonsense!" snapped Sandya. "That washing machine you ordered is Italian. Why didn't you ask Antonio to buy it for you?"

Sumitra came home. She had been looking forward all day to feeding washing into the machine, watching the clothes spin round and seeing the suds splashing against the "extra-large porthole." But she wasn't surprised when she found it wasn't there. Nothing ever seemed to be done quickly in their house. Her parents always went through devious channels, preferring to buy from someone they had known in Uganda, rather than from the local shops.

Bap phoned up the warehouse. "So sorry, so sorry," apologized Kirit. "My van is broken down. No deliveries this week. Next Monday, O.K.?"

The machine was finally delivered. For one month it stood in the front passage, protected by its cardboard wrapping, proclaiming *Made in Italy* in large square print. They began to use the top of the carton as a shelf, until one day Ela asked, "Bap, when can we use the machine?"

Bap had forgotten all about it. He had promised to buy his wife a machine and he had done so. He called for scissors and cut off the wire strips. The cardboard wrapping fell off—Ela and Bimla pounced on the packaging and took it upstairs to make a Wendy House.

The rest of the family gathered around the machine, admiring it anew. "Family Wash," muttered Mai, looking surprised. "What does it mean?" She had visions of them all jumping in and being washed Ganges-clean.

Sumitra laughed. "I'll write down what the programs mean in Gujarati once it's connected."

"I'm trying to remember a plumber I know," Bap said thoughtfully. "Wasn't there someone who moved to Leicester . . . ?"

"Bap!" exclaimed Sumitra. "Look, we got a ten-pound discount on the machine because we vaguely knew the warehouse manager, but how much was the delivery charge?"

"How much, how much—about eleven pounds?"

"Exactly, and they deliver free in Muswell Hill. Now you want to get a plumber from Leicester, when it's quicker and cheaper to find one locally. I'll look in the Yellow Pages and find somebody."

"Wait, wait," ordered Bap, "first I'll ask at the temple."

On Sunday after the prayers, he inquired if anyone knew a plumber. Mohan knew someone who was in India on a short trip and would not return till the following month. "Good, good," said Bap. "There is no hurry." He didn't have to do the washing. So for another month the machine stood exposed to the dust and was admired and stroked lovingly each morning until fingerprints marred the shiny chrome and Ela was told to take a cloth and polish it again.

The plumber returned from holiday. He turned out to be an electrician, but he said he knew enough about pipes to plumb in a washing machine. He arrived on Saturday morning with his electric drill and bored two holes through the kitchen wall. Then he measured the machine and found it was too large to fit under the low kitchen shelf. He went out whistling and returned with Polyfilla. The holes were filled up.

"Machine too big for kitchen, where you want him? You can keep in hall if you like, yes? Everyone seeing you have nice machine, you rich peoples."

No one responded to this suggestion. He tried again. "Washing machine in lounge. Very unusual. Nice. You know others with machine in lounge? Very classy. Setting trends!"

But Mai didn't want the washing machine in the lounge. The plumber sighed. He wished he hadn't taken this job. He was doing them a favor and they were being so fussy.

"Dining room," Bap said firmly. "Washing machine in dining room."

So it was decided. Two holes were bored through the dining-room wall to the water supply and the hose pipes fitted. The plumber was paid and then went back to being an electrician.

When they put the washing in that evening, sitting down to eat at the same time so they could observe the show, water began to pour out of the extra-large-capacity tub.

"Monty Python doesn't know what he's missing," Sumitra muttered to Sandya as she ran to phone the local plumber.

Later that night, as the washing machine was being repaired by a chirpy plumber with a cigarette behind his ear, Sumitra suddenly remembered that she hadn't looked up *pomme de pin*. She took down her dictionary and saw, with relief, that it meant fir cone, after all.

CHAPTER XIII

The hall was hushed. Sumitra lifted the guitar, pushed her long hair behind her back, strummed an introduction and began to sing. Her voice rang out clear and sweet, the audience hung on every word. In the front row, a woman sobbed with emotion.

As the song ended, the audience rose with one accord, cheering and applauding wildly. Sumitra bowed, turned to walk off the stage, but they would not let her go. "Sing it again!" they yelled. "More, more!" She smiled and began to play another tune.

"Belt up, Sumitra," shouted Sandya from the next room, banging crossly on the wall. "I'm trying to do my homework!" Mai was calling up the stairs, "Come and help me, stop playing that guitar. I wish Martin had never given it to you!"

Sumitra closed her eyes as the anger spluttered like a firecracker inside her. The vision of headlines reading: "Sue Patel Takes New York by Storm! Beautiful Girl Singer from London, England, an Overnight Success!" faded, and she strummed three angry chords before throwing the guitar on her bed. She went downstairs to exchange the sweet smell of success for the acrid fumes of boiling *ghee.*

As she fried the rounds her mother rolled out, a huge wave of misery engulfed her. Hilary and Lynne had gone to a local college dance, while Cinderella Patel remained at home, reeking of oil and dry flour. She turned suddenly and looked at Mai. "Do you like cooking?" she asked, wondering how her mother could bear this life, day after day.

Mai was bewildered. "What questions you ask!" she replied. "I don't know. Women cook for their families. You must help me and learn to cook for your own family. You are sixteen. Soon we must start thinking about looking for a husband. It is good you have passed your exams. You will marry well!"

Sumitra's tongue stuck to her mouth like an uncooked lump of dough. She turned the *poori* deftly as her mind screamed, "Never, never, never!" in the kitchen of her brain. The words of a pop song sizzled in the fat:

> *And all the songs I was going to sing, I'll never sing them now.*

And all the bells I was going to ring, I'll never ring them now.
And all the lives I was going to live
And all the loves I was going to give,
I'll never live them now,
I'll never give them now.

Mai patted her arm, leaving a floury impression like a palm print decorating a temple. "It's all right," she said with unusual gentleness. "It is the custom. You'll get used to the idea, there's no need to be shy. We all get used to it."

It had never occurred to Mai that her daughters might be questioning their way of life. Despite their smart clothes and the fact that at the weekends they wore sweaters and jeans like any other teen-ager, she was sure that their attitudes and conventions were Indian. She had never sat down and thought about it; she never thought about her children as separate entities. When she told Bap that she was worried about them, she meant that she was concerned that they would take suitable jobs, choose the right friends, marry decent partners. The criterion in each case was whether or not she would approve of their choice. So Mai was part of the Banquo line, carefully bequeathing to her children the ideas and philosophies that had been bequeathed to her. The fact that these conventions had evolved in different ages and in different countries was immaterial.

Mai never doubted that the girls would lead their lives in the same way as she lived hers, marrying someone carefully chosen by the parents, bearing children who would, of course, speak Gujarati and Hindi. She had no reason to doubt it when all around her she saw other cultures passing on their various truths to their own children and carefully isolating them from the British tradition in which they lived. She had seen synagogues, mosques, Greek and Russian Orthodox churches, and behind each of these institutions was a subculture energetically devoted to keeping a particular tradition alive.

Mai, like thousands of other mothers of minority groups, had many ways of perpetuating tradition. There was emotional, social and financial pressure. Thus the little dictatorships of family life flourished in the British democracy. Children were unhappy, rejected their parents' demands temporarily, made their heroic gestures, but were usually defeated by the sanctions imposed. Mothers wept, fathers talked of sacrifices, grandparents disapproved, and the son or daughter conceded and was sucked back into the family group.

Life continued as it had always done. The shrine was cleaned and polished, sandalwood paste prepared. Offerings were left for the gods, and roses decorated the ceremonial place. The girls plaited Gopal and Jayant braids at Rakshabandhan in order to ensure their health and happiness. They all went to the temple and, occasionally, to Indian films and dances.

As long as the outside culture remained beyond her house, Mai was content. The letters and notes from the alien society were ignored as if they had no right to be there. Requests to attend school functions or parents' evenings were left unanswered. What could she or Bap do at school? She trusted the teachers to do their job and, besides, she couldn't speak English. So she lived in her comfortable cocoon, only venturing out to go to work and surrounding herself with the friends she had known in Uganda.

Sumitra and some of her Indian friends, however, were beginning to resent the tight community laws. They objected to being relegated to the Bottom Division at the back of the temple. As sexual objects, women distracted the men from their prayers, so the men prayed while the women sat behind the barrier and gossiped. Then the women went to the communal kitchen to prepare food for the men. This division of labor annoyed the girls, who at school were encouraged to be independent, thoughtful, integrated, and at home to be docile, submissive and dutiful. Sumitra had to listen to the adults decrying the British way of life, while being educated into it herself.

Sumitra and her parents lived under the same roof without speaking to each other. Of course they talked; they spoke about the things that did not matter, but about the serious business of the meaning of life they were silent. There was no point of contact, and any questioning was called disobedience and would cause a scene. So Sumitra acted one part at home and another at school, and was never sure which role was really hers.

Sometimes events on the news reached out and touched them. Incidents of growing racial tension in Notting Hill, Birmingham, Southall. The places were different but the causes were the same: a lack of government awareness and initiative and an unfriendly host population causing the immigrants to turn in on themselves. One side felt threatened, the other rebuffed.

Sumitra felt all these pressures. One part of her wanted to live as an Indian girl, carrying on the great traditions and culture, while another part of her wanted to participate in Western freedom. On the one hand, they read of incidents in Southall, of young Asians being attacked and even murdered. This made them fearful, retreating into the group. These racial incidents defined certain boundaries between the immigrants and host society, and caused Bap to give his weekly lecture on the superiority of their own way of life.

On the other hand, there were occasionally reports in the paper about young Asian girls killing themselves because they had not wanted to go through with an arranged marriage, or because the strain of living two lives was overwhelming. As she watched yet another *poori* puff up and turn brown, Sumitra wondered if that was the only way out. She had often wished lately that she were dead.

The next morning Sumitra woke early from a restless sleep and lay in bed dully staring at the cracked plaster patterns on the ceiling. She heard squeals and thumps as Ela and Bimla chased each other round their bedroom. The sunlight fell through the curtain. Sumitra closed her eyes. The thought of life closing around her was stifling. She felt once more like a figure in a glass bubble, shaken in all directions by some huge hand that controlled her future.

A car hooted outside. "Shut up! Go away and leave me alone!" she shouted. The doorbell rang. Muttering angrily, she pulled on some clothes and went downstairs. Ela had already opened the door, and Martin, Maria and Sally were standing in the front hall.

"Come on!" Martin said. "Hurry up and get ready! It's a beautiful day and we're going to Littlehampton."

Ela dashed off to tell Mai. "I'm so glad to see you," Sumitra beamed. "I'll make coffee and get some food together." She bustled round happily wrapping food in paper bags, while Sally related the fight she had had with Ben at nursery.

They piled into the car, Mai with Sally on her lap, Maria squashed between Ela and Bimla. Bap stayed at home, glad of a peaceful day. The bank-holiday traffic was heavy and Martin's car overheated so they had to keep stopping, but they laughed and joked and sang their way to the coast.

Finding a sheltered spot on the beach, they unpacked the picnic. As usual when they all went out, there was a mixture of English and Indian food. Egg sandwiches, *chapatis*, tomato rolls, *pooris*, crisps, *chevra*, *samosas*, and bread pudding. The young children ran about collecting stones and seashells. Sandya paddled in the sea, the wind blowing her dress against her thin figure, like one of Lowry's matchstick ladies. Sumitra tucked up her jeans and went to join her. She felt warm, contented and at peace. Martin strode off into the distance, making for the headland.

Maria grinned at Mai. “It’s lovely, isn’t it? I love the seaside. I said to Martin we should all go out today.”

“Fine.” Mai smiled back.

Maria put her hand onto the sand. She lifted her fingers and watched the golden grains trickle out. “Do you know what this is called?”

“I don’t know.”

“Sand,” said Maria.

“Sand,” repeated Mai.

Maria picked up a shell. “Shell,” she said.

“Shell,” Mai repeated.

Maria sighed. “I really must start giving you English lessons once a week.” Despite her intentions, she still hadn’t got round to keeping her promise. She had bought a book for teaching English to foreign students, but with the excitement of the wedding, it still lay unopened in its wrapper. “I’ll start next week.”

Mai smiled. She closed her eyes. It felt good sitting in the warmth and feeling the sun shining on her. It was like Uganda with the sea glistening and the children playing around them.

Sumitra and Sandya ran back, laughing and shaking cold water over them. They flopped on the sand. “Any food left?” asked Sumitra. “I’m starving!”

“I wish we’d brought a ball,” said Ela, running up.

“I’ve got one somewhere in this bag,” said Maria, rummaging through her basket. They all played football until Martin came back, windswept and his face burned by the sun.

“Come on, we’re off!” he announced.

“No, no!” squealed the little girls. “Not yet, we’ve only just come!”

“We’re going on a speedboat.” He laughed. “Of course, if you don’t want to come . . .” The rest of the sentence was drowned in whoops of joy. He led them down to the pier, running ahead with the younger children, while Sandya and Sumitra gazed in shop windows and Mai and Maria followed sedately.

Mai hung back from the boat. "Come on!" Maria insisted, pulling her arm, "it's lovely."

"I no like," Mai faltered.

"Come on, Mai," said Sandya.

Mai sat gingerly on one of the seats, pulling her sari tightly around herself. Maria sat next to her, holding her arm. The wind tore through their hair, the spray stung their eyes. The boat lifted its prow to the wind, racing through the water. No sooner had the ride finished than Ela cried, "Can we have another go, Mai, please?"

"Of course you can't," scolded Sandya. "Don't be so greedy!"

Mai looked in her purse. It was good to see the girls enjoying themselves so much. "You want again? Bimla, Maria, Sandya?" They shook their heads and disembarked.

"Here, Sumitra, take her round again." Mai gave her the money.

"You ought to get a season ticket," commented the boatman as he swung the boat away. "Hold on."

The two girls clasped the rail. Sumitra willed the boat to go faster—the speed was exhilarating and mind-deadening. It was impossible to feel worried or tense with the air whipping her cheeks and hair flying around her face. Closing her eyes, she let her tensions be swept away by the wind.

It was funny how different things seemed. Yesterday everything was difficult and dreary. Now, because Martin had taken them out for the day, nothing seemed the same. It was a matter of perspective. When they went up the Thames on an outing, things changed depending on where she was standing: looking down at a boat from a bridge, or looking across from the banks, or on the boat waving at people on the riverside. Yet she was the same person no matter where she stood.

Now she was conscious of the others watching her and Ela from the shore. Glancing through her lids against the salt spray, she felt her little sister's warm hand in hers and could just make out the laughing group on the quayside, waiting for the boat to come in. *If only I could stay here forever*, she thought, *whizzing round and round in increasing circles, never reaching land.* The boat dropped speed and slowed in to moor. Ela squeezed her fingers. "Wasn't that terrific!"

Ela dashed up the steps to Bimla. "That was great, even better than the first time! You should have come." Turning to Maria she said, "Bimla's scared. She was scared on the plane, and she's scared of boats, too. She's a real coward!"

"I'm not a coward!" Bimla retaliated indignantly. "You should see Ela when we come out of school. She hides behind me when the boys call us names!"

They all began walking into town. Maria stopped to fasten Sally's anorak; Ela and Bimla waited with her. "What do you mean? Who calls you names?"

"The boys from Finchley Down."

"What do they call you?" Maria asked.

"Oh, just, you know, things like Paki, and Blackie, and stuff like that."

Maria stopped walking and Sally tugged impatiently at her hand. "That's awful," said Maria. "Doesn't anyone tell them off?"

"Once a man told them off, but usually nobody seems to hear."

"Martin's got a friend who works at Finchley Down. I'll ask him to see what he can do about it."

They ran to catch up with the others. They trooped into the town and headed for Mario's coffee bar. Martin ordered coffee, cakes and ice cream. Mai looked happy and carefree, Ela and Bimla were tired and laughing, Sandya and Sumitra were busy teasing Martin. Sally spread chocolate cream all round her face, and Mai wiped it off with a tissue.

We're like a big family, Maria thought, all different types and ages, but all bound together by a bond of affection.

She grinned to herself. "What are you laughing at?" asked Martin. Maria smiled at him. Sumitra felt a pang of envy as she saw the understanding glance they exchanged. They were so happy; she was glad for Maria's sake, but although Maria always told her that nothing had changed, she was always welcome, somehow their togetherness emphasized her own isolation.

Bimla stuffed the rest of her éclair into her mouth. "Don't forget it's my birthday next week!" she reminded them, scattering crumbs all over the table.

"You better eat a bit slower or you'll choke before then!" said Martin.

"Anyway, we couldn't forget," added Maria, "you've been reminding us for months!"

Sumitra had ordered a cake from the shop around the corner, and she and Mai had been busily baking biscuits and mounds of food. Motiben, Leela, Jayant and little Trupti were coming, too.

On Sunday, Sumitra and Sandya set the food out in the lounge. The cake proclaimed in blue icing HAPPY BIRTHDAY, BIMLA. Motiben and the rest of the family arrived soon after lunch and gave Bimla her presents. Ela pressed her face to the window, looking for Martin's car. "Here they are!" she yelled as it came down the street. Maria waved as she and Sally carried out brightly wrapped parcels from the boot.

Bimla and Ela rushed to the door. "Come in, come in!" Bimla urged. "Jayant bought me a desk and Sumitra got me some pens and a birthday cake and Sandya gave me a pencil case and Ela made me a cat out of felt and Mai . . ."

"Let them come in first!" laughed Sandya, coming up behind and rescuing them from one of Bimla's unending sentences. "Come in and sit down. You know everyone, don't you?"

They went into the lounge. Sally toddled up to the loaded table and grabbed a sandwich. Maria caught her up and led her away. "Wait until you're asked," she said.

Bimla opened her parcels. There was a painting book from Sally and some oil paints from Maria. Martin produced an easel. Bimla hugged her friends. "Thanks, thank you. I really wanted some paints and an easel. Mrs. Johnson says I should be an artist. I think I will, too."

Mai and Sumitra handed round the food, and they all sat on the floor eating and talking. The birthday candles were lit. Sally pulled Mai over to the window. "Curtains. Must pull curtains, like at nursery." Mai pulled the curtains and they sang "Happy Birthday" in English and Gujarati, and cheered as Bimla blew out the candles.

"Good, good," said Jayant, throwing Ela into the air. "You are getting big, too, aren't you?"

Bap put on some Indian records and they sat round tapping their feet. Sumitra sat down on the floor near Maria. "Isn't it your birthday soon, Sumitra?" asked Leela. "You'll be seventeen, won't you? What are you going to do?"

"She's coming to work in my shop," Jayant said. "There's a job ready for her."

Jayant's shop was in a busy road in Edgware. He sold sweets, cigarettes and magazines, and needed another pair of hands. Sumitra looked at her parents. "I want to stay on at school," she mumbled, embarrassed. "I'm not sure what I'm going to do yet." One thing she was sure about. She was not going to work for Jayant. She was going to be an air hostess, but had not yet mentioned this at home. She had talked about it to her friends at school, but until she knew what qualifications were necessary, she had no intention of seeing her plans squashed. Her parents would be delighted if she worked with

Jayant, but Sumitra wanted something wider than that for herself. She wanted to step outside her daily routine and see new things, meet new people.

"Sumitra ought to stay at school," Maria supported her. "If she does A-levels, she'll have more opportunities open to her."

"Opportunities, opportunities," scoffed Jayant. "She is a woman. What does she want opportunities for? All she needs is a husband. I am offering her a good job till she finds one."

Maria caught Sumitra's eye. What Jayant was telling her was to mind her own business.

Sally saved the moment of awkward silence by pouring her orange juice over Trupti. Trupti howled. Maria dashed out to get a cloth and the moment passed.

CHAPTER XIV

Even before he had married her, Martin knew that Maria was one of the worst cooks in the world. They had soon come to an amicable agreement about the housework. On weekdays Maria prepared convenience foods, and most weekends Martin cooked the lunch. They also shared the household chores. Sumitra had been surprised one day to find Martin sweeping the stairs, while Maria and Sally were washing up. "My dad never helps at home," she exclaimed. "Your mum's a good housewife, that's why!" commented Martin as he busily swept clouds of dust into the pan. "Maria calls it Women's Lib, all our role sharing, but I call it self-preservation."

"He doesn't mean it," put in Maria. "Martin just pretends

he's an MCP. But he's really quite liberated beneath his grim exterior! Anyway it makes sense; we both go out to work, so why shouldn't we both help at home?"

One Saturday in late summer, they invited Sumitra to lunch. Maria had cooked the meal, wanting to impress her husband and friend. She had followed a recipe for lemoned chicken. The table was neatly laid, with a small jug of fresh flowers from the garden in the middle. Maria proudly served up the meal, ignoring the fact that the diners were sniffing the air in despairing anticipation. She set the plates in front of them. "This is really nice. It's a Greek dish, quite a delicacy."

Sally took a mouthful and grimaced. "It's nasty, Mummy," she whimpered.

"Don't be rude!" snapped Maria. "Eat it up, it's lovely!" She sat down and took a mouthful herself, choked and began to laugh. Sumitra gingerly swallowed a morsel. She had never tasted anything so awful. The cream and lemon had curdled, and the chicken tasted like rotten fish. Martin looked at them all in annoyance.

"That's enough!" he scolded. "Eat it up! You types are so fussy—there are people starving and there you are complaining!" He pushed a huge forkful into his mouth while they all watched. He began to cough. "Maria, I think this must be the most revolting meal you've ever cooked!"

They all burst out laughing. "Go on, Martin, eat it up!" Sumitra encouraged him. "There are starving people in the world who'd be glad of that!"

"No way. I think they'd prefer a check!" Martin began to take the plates off the table and scoop the contents into the garbage.

As they hastily made jam sandwiches, Martin asked Sumitra how she was getting on at school. "School's a drag," Sumitra told him. "Honestly, it's so boring. Most of the teachers treat us like babies—well, not all of them," she added hastily as

Martin opened his mouth to object. "I must admit that some are O.K., but I wish I could work at Hanbury's all the time. Mike's introduced me to some of his mates and we all go down to the pub at lunchtime. One of the boys—Roger—comes from New Zealand and he's really interesting. He knows all about Maoris and we've been to museums with some other friends a couple of times."

"You want to watch it," warned Martin. "If your dad finds out—"

"I know, I think he'd kill me, but I've just got to the stage where I feel I've got to go where I want to sometimes, with people I want to go out with."

"Of course you do, love," sympathized Maria, handing out coffee and cakes.

"Did you make these?" Martin asked suspiciously.

"No, I bought them!"

Sighing with relief, Martin and Sumitra helped themselves.

"You're seventeen, aren't you?" Maria went on. "If you can't enjoy yourself at your age, then there's not much point, is there?"

"Oh, Maria," sighed Sumitra as she put on her jacket to go back to work. "If only you were my mother!"

As she journeyed back on the 263 bus, Sumitra felt happy and lighthearted. Maria and Martin always cheered her up. Martin had teased her, calling her a teen-age trendy because recently she'd been buying magazines and trying to dress in the latest fashions. What she didn't learn from the magazines, however, was what kind of makeup to use on her skin, how to accentuate her eyes, what sort of lipstick to apply. It wasn't that the magazines did not give beauty hints—they were full of little else. It was just that every weekly journal ignored the fact that there were millions of people living in Britain of Indian, West Indian, Chinese or Eastern origin. Fashion seemed only to apply to girls with white skin and mid-brown hair.

So Sumitra experimented alone, spending hours in the bathroom, trying gold or silver eyeshadow, mixing shades, putting different-color reds on her lips, till one of the others knocked angrily on the door. One day while she was locked away with her pots of creams and lotions, she heard muffled giggles outside and went out to find that Ela and Bimla had scribbled a notice saying SUMITRA'S BEAUTY SALON and hung it over the doorknob.

On Saturdays Sumitra became Sue, in swinging skirts and bright blouses, with a tailored jacket tossed casually over her shoulders. She wore her hair loose, hanging down her back. From nine to five, Sue was liberated, smart and cheeky, like the other girls at work. Sue was part of the adult world, responsible for running the office while the rest of the staff served in the shop. The adding machine, the switchboard, the typewriter, all these were part of her domain, and she enjoyed being mistress of this little kingdom, if only for one day a week. And the feel of crisp pound notes, five at the end of the day now, never failed to surprise and delight her. She thought of the other members of staff as old friends, and all the while she was secretly putting some money into the post office. This represented her independence. Half her wages were given to her mother to help out at home, while she saved the rest for buying clothes and gifts. But in the post office, PO Account 96124XZY, she had over the last few years accumulated the sum of forty-five pounds.

At lunchtime Pat and Peter accompanied her to the nearby sandwich bar or to the pub. As Peter and Sumitra passed for eighteen, no one questioned that they might be drinking illegally. Pat remarked that since she was fifty but looked sixty, she more than made up for them. So although Bap continued his tirades against the evils of drink and tobacco, his daughter often sat in a den of iniquity called the Five Feathers, not far from Tally Ho Corner, eating a plowman's lunch, drinking lemon and lime, smoking a couple of cigarettes.

Sitting in the pub at lunchtime was one of the highlights of the week. Mike had been transferred to one of the firm's branches at Brent Cross. But his friend Roger and his traveling companions often came into the Five Feathers. Sometimes Sumitra accompanied them on Sundays to the Tate Gallery, the Science Museum, or an afternoon concert, telling Mai that she was spending the day at Lynne's.

She had found out that to be an air hostess you had to be 5′4″, of sound body and mind, physically attractive and twenty-one years old. The more subjects she could get at O- and A-level, the easier it would be to break into an oversubscribed profession. All she could do, then, was wait to be twenty-one.

Sometimes she wondered how she would manage to live on her own, after being part of a large, close-knit family, yet felt she had to make the break. Anyway, it all seemed so far away, too distant to worry about.

Because she was happier now, she found that people appeared to be nice to her. Mai left her alone as long as the housework was done. Sandya helped her with the chores, and with a fuller social life, home did not seem as constricting as it had before. Sumitra lived in a magic bubble, insulated from all harm.

The last person she would have expected to burst that bubble was Leela. Since the birth of Trupti, they had talked about many things, about life in Uganda, in England, about racism, about the future. On many subjects Leela agreed with Sumitra and advised her, "Don't let them push you into an early marriage. There's plenty of time for that, especially for a beautiful girl like you. Don't, don't marry at eighteen, for you will have the rest of your life ahead as the slave of a man and his family."

"Leela, aren't you happy with Jayant?" Sumitra asked, saddened.

"I am not happy, I am not unhappy." Leela shrugged. "I did

what seemed right. When we were in Uganda, everyone married young. It was the custom. It is only here, now, I see many women staying single till they are twenty-five or twenty-six, some choosing not to marry at all, that I think my life has been spoiled. But then, other women seem happy, some husbands are more helpful than mine, more Western than Jayant. If we had not come, I would not have thought like this."

Trupti put one sticky hand on her mother's sari, and with the other pulled at Sumitra's skirt. "That's the trouble, isn't it?" Sumitra mused. "We did come."

So it was by an unhappy coincidence that one Saturday morning, almost four months after Sumitra had first met the New Zealanders, Leela and Jayant were driving back from their weekly shopping jaunt just as Sumitra and her friends walked into the Five Feathers. "Look, Jayant," said Leela conversationally, "isn't that Sumitra?" Jayant looked, saw their niece entering the pub and screeched his car to a halt. An angry blare from the car behind brought him back to his senses. He found a parking space and jumped out. "Stay here!" he ordered his wife.

Jayant was full of his own sense of righteousness. As a young male, the honor of the family rested on his shoulders. Sumitra was walking round with a crowd of white boys, and she was going into a pub!

He stormed into the Five Feathers. The acrid smell of beer and cigarettes hit him like a slap. He drew himself up and looked around. She was sitting with her friends in a corner, lighting a cigarette with a drink of orange juice in front of her. "Sumitra!" he screamed.

She looked up, startled. "Whatever are you doing here, Jayant?" she asked, her heart beating very fast. "Would you like a drink?"

"You trying to be funny? Since when does a good Hindu go into a pub? Come home, come home at once!" he shouted.

Sumitra shut her eyes. She felt as if she had been waiting all her life for this moment, as if the answer she had been searching for were about to be revealed. "No, I won't come home," she said. "How did you know I was here?"

"Never mind how I knew, you are coming home!" He took her arm, pulled her from her seat and dragged her up. She stumbled and fell over Roger's feet. Roger steadied her.

"Now wait a minute," said Roger. "What do you think you're doing? Sue's with me and I don't think she's ready to go yet."

Sumitra looked at them both, hating every minute of the ridiculous scene.

The landlord came over and asked Jayant to leave. "Sorry, love," he said to Sumitra. "You're always welcome in here, but not him." He jerked his thumb at Jayant in contempt. "Get out and don't come in again making a disturbance! This young lady never causes any trouble, and I don't like shouting in here."

"Did you know she's only seventeen?" yelled Jayant. "You're breaking the law, selling liquor to a minor!"

"I'm going," said Sumitra. "I've had enough of all this."

They all left the pub and found Leela outside on the pavement, calling to Jayant to come back and leave Sumitra alone. Jayant started shouting again, waving his fist threateningly at Sumitra. He tried to push her into the car, but Roger prevented him. "Home, home, I'm taking you home!" he shouted again and again. Passersby were looking at them.

Roger tried to calm Jayant down. Sumitra couldn't bear it any longer. She broke away from the arguing group and ran down the street to the sanctuary of the office.

Pat had gone to lunch early that day and was now sorting out some stock in the shop. "What's the matter, love?" she asked as Sumitra returned in tears.

In between great painful sobs, Sumitra told her what had happened. "He hates white people, he can't understand that I want to mix with everyone, that I don't think as he does. He wants me to be like him, but I can't. Now he's ruining my life. I hate him!"

Pat put her arms round the girl. "There, ducks," she comforted. "Don't take it so hard. All youngsters have arguments with their families. I had enough when I was young, I should know. Me mum didn't want me to marry Alf, didn't think he was good enough, and every night there were argy bargies and rows loud enough to be heard in the next borough. But I married my Alf and I've been happy all these years. You stick up for yourself, dear, and don't take no notice of anyone else. You show 'em!" And she bustled off into the little kitchen to fetch Sumitra a cup of tea.

"You know, Sue," she said as she came back, "you've changed a lot in the time you've worked here. When you came, you were a little girl, so polite and, I dunno, sort of reserved. But you've become cheeky and bright, and in the last few weeks you've seemed much happier. Don't let that clever dick uncle of yours spoil anything."

Pat chattered on, consoling and cheering. Sumitra stopped crying, and Pat left her to attend to a customer. Sumitra studied the pile of correspondence in front of her. But she couldn't concentrate. What would Jayant do? She could just imagine the scene at home. Jayant would make her out to be a prostitute and an alcoholic. Mai would be shocked. Bap would be furious. She knew she would return home that evening to a terrible scene, a scene that had been brewing for months. She couldn't go home that night. They all needed time to get the whole affair into perspective.

What it all boiled down to was the fact that she wanted more freedom than they were prepared to allow her. She was over seventeen, almost entitled to vote. But as a citizen of what? If she was a British citizen, then in a few months' time she would be legally entitled to speak to whom she liked, eat what she liked, wear what she liked, and drink what she liked. If she was an Indian citizen, then she would be inhibited in what she did.

She did not want to choose, she wanted to bridge both cultures, taking the best from both, the tradition and discipline of the one and the freedom and choice of the other. But they would not let her do this. If she stayed at home, she would have to be Indian through and through, agree to an arranged marriage, live an arranged life making arranged *samosas* in an arranged kitchen for the rest of her arranged years. If she left home, she would be alone, perhaps rejected by the very society she wanted to join. How could anyone decide between being alone or being submerged? It was an impossible decision to make.

All Sumitra knew was that she could not return home that night. But where could she go? She thought of Maria; Maria had always said that she could stay there. But Maria and Martin were not just her friends, but friends of the whole family. Maria and Martin were her parents' sole contact with the English community on a social level. It wasn't fair to break that contact.

Sumitra suddenly thought of Lynne. Lynne had left school a year ago and was now studying at Art College. She found the phone number in her bag and rang up. Lynne wasn't there. "Mrs. Baker," Sumitra said to Lynne's mother, trying to keep her voice steady, "I'm really sorry to bother you, but something awful's happened. Please, can I stay at your place tonight?"

"Of course you can, my dear," said Mrs. Baker. "Don't tell me about it now—what time do you finish work? We'll come and pick you up. It will be so nice to see you again."

At five, Lynne and her mother were waiting outside the shop. "Don't worry, Sumitra," said Mrs. Baker as they listened to her story on the way back. "As soon as we get home, you can phone your mother and tell her where you are. Then I'll drive you back tomorrow morning and try to sort it out with her. Just imagine, all you've done is to have a glass of fruit juice in a pub with some friends. I'll make her see, don't worry."

Sumitra *was* worried. She knew that Mai would not understand. When Lynne's mother put it like that, it was so simple. But that was the trouble with words. You could wrap up a situation or a story and say, "That was it, that is what happened, that's all," but it wouldn't be all, only a tiny part of it. It was as if everyone were using different alphabets, different sound systems. There were some words that Mai would never be able to pronounce in English because they were sounds that could not be represented in Gujarati. There were sounds that English people could not make in French and vice versa, because they couldn't hear the difference.

Every single person was operating in his own alphabetical universe, but the letters existing in one did not exist in another, so they could only get the general gist of the meaning, not the delicate nuances. To Mrs. Baker, all Sumitra had done was to have a glass of orange juice in a pub with some friends. To Mai and Bap, what she had done was to disgrace the family name by disobeying the rules, the laws that said that Hindu girls should not go into pubs, should always be chaperoned, should never smoke. And the two different versions, the two different scripts, would never be reconciled.

CHAPTER XV

Sumitra spent most of that night talking to Lynne and Mrs. Baker. She phoned home and told Mai where she was. Mai started screaming hysterically over the phone while Sumitra tried to explain that she had only gone into the pub for a drink and a chat. "I'll see you tomorrow," Sumitra told her, and put the phone down, feeling shaky and sick. Lynne was excited. It was like a play: beautiful heroine, wicked parents. But to Sumitra it was as if some dreary drama she had been watching all her life had unfolded another scene before her.

Lynne's mother was an expert in community relations, having worked voluntarily in this field for years. "It will be all right, dear," she kept saying. "They just need time to readjust. Girls of your age are a handful no matter where their parents come from. They probably haven't realized that you are grown up now. Give them time."

Sumitra smiled wearily. Mrs. Baker was very kind, but she didn't really understand the situation. To her, community relations was a matter of getting people to smile at their foreign neighbors, encouraging people of different races to go to cultural evenings and lectures. Mrs. Baker and people like her demanded that all groups have the freedom to express themselves as they wished. The idea of allowing people within those groups to deviate from tradition did not come into the picture at all. Once again, Sumitra felt she had reached an impasse—no one completely understood what it was she needed or wanted.

She sat in silence as Mrs. Baker drove her home the following day. "I'll come in with you, there's no need to worry," Lynne's mother said as they pulled up outside the rose-covered walls. Sumitra noted dully that the flowers were losing some of their petals and that the leaves were turning brown. She walked up the path feeling as if she were outside her own body, looking on. Mrs. Baker rang the bell. Bap threw open the door and began to shout, but seeing the Englishwoman with his daughter, he stopped. He silently ushered them into the front room. This was rarely used, so it gave the meeting an added note of somberness.

The family court was assembled. For the prosecution—Bap, Mai, Jayant. For the defense—Sumitra, Sandya and Mrs. Baker. Ela and Bimla had been sent to Motiben to escape from the evil influence of their wicked sister. "We don't want them perverted," Mai had wept the night before. "They must go away!" So the two younger girls had spent the night at Highgate, where they would be spared the unpleasantness that everyone knew had to follow.

Bap began the proceedings. "Jayant saw you going into the pub. He saw you drinking vodka. He saw you with English boys. You spent a night away from home. You have brought shame on your family. We will never get you and your sisters good husbands now. See what you have done, see what you have caused!"

He continued his sermon while Sumitra mentally counted the squares on the patterned wallpaper. There were seven across and four down, then a little flower, then seven across and four down. Seven fours were twenty-eight; there were fifty patterns across the length of the wall; twenty-eight times fifty equaled one thousand four hundred. There was a spot of grease on one of the petals of the flowers. Bap wouldn't let them decorate as the home was temporary, although the girls had offered to buy the paint and do it themselves. She half-listened to the words. *Vodka.* She had not been drinking vodka, but it didn't matter. It wasn't the drink that was important, although alcohol was forbidden. She might have been drinking water for all they cared. It was the fact that she was stepping outside the community circle.

"Mr. Patel," Lynne's mother interrupted, bored with the angry flow of Gujarati. She was the committee woman now, brisk and efficient, overriding a verbose speaker. "Obviously I don't understand what you're saying, but I gather you are very cross with your daughter. It really is quite simple. Sumitra is seventeen, nearly an adult in the eyes of the law. You really must allow her a bit more freedom. I do understand your problem; I have a girl of my own, always wanting to go out, to buy smart clothes, to go her own way. But all Sumitra has done is to have a drink with some friends and spend the night with me." She flashed him a charming smile, as if to commiserate with him about the difficulties of looking after children who were already grown up.

"Don't listen, don't listen!" shouted Jayant, the chief witness. "Sumitra has disgraced the temple, disgraced the family, disgraced me!" *Now we're coming to it,* Sumitra thought. *Just because Jayant's a big shot in the temple he thinks he's got to push his views down everyone's throat.* "Don't listen to white people, they are all rotten, they only use you!"

Lynne's mother flushed. Beads of sweat appeared on her brow and she pulled at the string of pearls she wore around her throat. "I'd better go now, dear," she said to Sumitra. "I've some guests coming for lunch. If there's any real trouble, just ring us and I'll be back at once." She gave Jayant a long, cold look as she left the room. They listened to the door closing and heard the car drive away.

The trial recommenced. So far Sumitra had not spoken. There was no need. She was already tried and found guilty, it only remained to see what sentence would be passed. Mai cried, Bap shouted, Jayant screamed. Sumitra now tried to explain. "All I did was have a drink of orange juice." To her amazement, her voice was calm and reasonable, the others sounded like cackling ducks. "O.K., I did have a cigarette. I won't do it again. Yes, I was with some boys, but so what? They are my friends. No, they are not Indian, but what about it? My heart is the same color as theirs. How can I only have Indian friends when we're living in England? That is hypocritical. And what about Maria and Martin? They're English, but you don't mind them coming round or taking us out."

"Don't let them come then," hissed Jayant. "They are white people. White people only take what they want."

"Don't be so silly," shouted Sandya. She had been listening in silence, hoping that Sumitra could get herself out of this trouble. Last night had been terrible. Alone with her parents, she had had to listen to lectures about the evils of going out with Englishmen, of drinking, of eating meat, of getting too friendly with white people, of smoking, all of which she knew Sumitra did. Sandya herself could now see that her life would be much the same as her sister's: one of work and social isolation and obedience, or of unavoidable conflict and argument. She had meant to keep out of this as much as possible, there was no point in getting everyone even more upset, but she couldn't allow Jayant to slander her friends.

"You are talking rubbish, Jayant! Maria teaches Mai English. Martin gives us lifts. They are our friends. We share things—they don't just take from us!" She stood glaring at him till Bap said, "Don't you dare talk to Jayant like that! Go upstairs to your room!"

Sandya went out, slamming the door.

Sumitra was left alone, the sinner among the just. It was first decided that they would send her to India to stay with relatives. It was then decided to send her to an aunt in Wolverton. It was finally decided to send her to Milton Keynes. It appeared to be vital that she be sent away, so that she would be saved from the bad influences around her, and so that her sisters would be saved from her anarchic tendencies. Sumitra let them talk. She felt drained and exhausted. None of it made sense to her, but it was clear that her brief period of happiness had come to an abrupt conclusion.

The next few weeks were tense and difficult. To her surprise and relief, Sandya was strongly on her side, and there were many arguments between parents and daughters. Ela and Bimla were allowed to return home after a couple of days, and Bimla sided with her parents, but Ela in her whimsical way took no notice of anyone. She drew a picture for Sumitra and left it on her bed. Sumitra was grateful. She sat morose and silent at meals and was forbidden to go out alone anymore.

Sandya was sent to work with her on Saturdays and had to sit reading in the office. She was detailed to accompany Sumitra home after school. "Honestly, I feel like a spy," she said. Sumitra's schoolwork suffered. She couldn't see any point in working hard when she knew that she would never be allowed to do what she wanted to. She had broached the subject tentatively with Mai, asking what they would think if she joined the airlines, but Mai had said no, she was going to work in Jayant's shop, so that they would know what she was up to. She had shown that she could not be trusted. They wanted her to work in the shop, come home at night, do the housework, cook the supper, marry someone of their choice, and stay home doing someone else's housework and cooking someone else's *samosas*. Therefore, she realized, there was no point in studying anymore.

Sumitra felt like an old woman whose life had already been lived. Her teachers asked what was wrong, told her she wouldn't pass her A-levels if she didn't try harder, but she couldn't speak to them. A plan was half-forming at the back of her mind, but she needed time to think about it.

The tension gradually lifted; the incident, if not forgotten, was never spoken about; but the parents and daughters had a new watchfulness about them. Not long afterward, a letter fell onto the hall mat. It was from India, from Dadima, Bap's mother. She wrote that she was coming to live in England, had at last obtained a passport and would be with them in a week.

They cleared out the front room, putting up a bed. Mai and Bap were pleased the old lady was going to make her home with them. This would be good for Sumitra; the grandmother would reinforce their wishes, put forth their point of view.

They all went to meet the plane. Jayant drove them to the airport and the girls waited excitedly as the passengers disembarked. An old woman in a white sari hobbled slowly across the arrival lounge. Bap went to embrace her, and then introduced the family. None of the girls had ever seen their grandmother before.

"I don't like her," whispered Ela to Bimla. "I can't understand what she says." The grandmother spoke a different, purer Gujarati, their own being corrupted with Swahili and Hindi words. Once home, she sat barefoot, one leg tucked beneath her, nodding at her grandchildren, smiling and talking about relatives and friends. After a few days, she made her presence felt. "Sumitra, you can't wear that dress. It's a bad dress. I can see your arms and your neck. Why don't you wear a sari?" Then she started on Sandya. "Why does your mother let you wear those shoes? They are so high, they are foolish shoes. Wear Indian sandals!" The little ones came in for her censure, too. "You have had your hair cut. That is bad. It is not the custom. You must grow it long again."

When Bap returned home after work, she would issue commands. "Girls, get your father's slippers! Make him some tea! Let him sit down there! Ah, he is tired." The girls were tired, too, but that did not seem to matter. So Bap was waited on even more than usual. When Jayant and Gopal came to visit, it was the same. "Give your uncle that bit, it is tastier. I will have the burnt piece. I am only a woman. He has not got enough. Take from my plate. Eat up, Jayant, you work so hard, you are looking tired. Let him rest now, there, there."

Soon Sumitra and Sandya were smarting under her harsh reign. Everything had to be done by the women for the men. The males were waited on hand and foot—it was the custom.

It was not the custom, however, to be waited on by young girls educated to feel equal to their brothers. The devoted slaves had been replaced by resentful servants. "No one has ever looked after us," Sandya said to Sumitra. "We've always looked after other people. Wouldn't it be great if just once we came home to a meal that had been cooked by someone else?" They both thought of the television ad for drinking-chocolate, and smiled wistfully.

"Hurry, hurry," called Dadima in her high quavering voice, "the men are waiting!"

"Let them wait," snarled Sumitra to herself.

Since her fall from grace, Sumitra had been unable to talk to Jayant. She hated and despised him. Although forced to cook for him from time to time, and serve him plates of food, nothing would induce her to look at him. She refused to visit Leela's house anymore; although she felt sorry for her aunt, she had only a cold contempt for the rest of her relatives. Jayant's attempts to jolly her out of her mood were unsuccessful. Sumitra simply stared through him as if he were a barrier in her way.

Now that Dadima had come, life was even more tedious than ever. There was even less time for studying with friends dropping in to visit the old lady. Each batch of visitors meant a fresh batch of *chapatis*.

"I never have a chance to speak to you anymore," Maria said one Sunday, helping Sumitra to roll out the dough. "I wish I could help you more, but I don't know what to do!"

"You help me when you teach my mum English," replied Sumitra, neatly dropping another round into the fat. "That gives me an hour's peace at least!"

Maria had finally got around to giving Mai lessons. She had no experience in teaching English, just the wish to allow Mrs. Patel to communicate with her neighbors. They had started off with a copy of an English magazine, but Maria had quickly been brought face-to-face with the difficulties of the English language plus the gap between the life portrayed in the magazine and the life she witnessed in Mrs. Patel's family.

"When Mary started school, I wept buckets," one heart-rending story began. It was impossible to explain how buckets could be wept to someone who didn't know what a bucket was. Each sentence involved long, complicated explanations, and Maria was never sure whether Mai understood or not. At first their lessons were like a catechism. "Do you understand?" Maria would ask, having explained at length that "shoplifting" did not mean picking up shops but was another word for stealing. "Stealing, you know, taking something that belongs to somebody else, do you understand?" Mai would smile, saying, "Understand, understand." "What does shoplifting mean?" Maria would inquire hopefully. Mai would smile and laugh, "I don't know!" Then Maria would laugh and turn to another page.

She rejected the story of a film star's action-packed life as being too shocking. There was a page on makeup, that looked more promising, but on second thoughts the advice didn't apply to her pupil. The models were all fair-skinned and golden-haired. She tried the fashion pages. "Fellas will be seeing a lot more of you at night this summer. . . ." This would only confirm her pupil's idea that English society was full of semi-naked women trying to catch a man.

There was no way that she could explain to a sensitive, cultured woman whose English was almost nonexistent that the magazines her daughters read only portrayed the most glamorous, the most exciting and the most shocking items. The media portrayed an image that very few people actually followed. She wanted to ask her, "Have you ever seen anyone wearing these clothes? This is only a cartoon of life," but there was this great linguistic divide between them. This was how it must seem to Mrs. Patel every day when she stepped out of her front door and was surrounded by people chattering and gossiping in a language she could not understand. Even when she had grasped the meaning of the words, she was still hampered by the fact that the word could mean something else in another context, or when used colloquially. Maria was inspired by this realization to hurry on, to open the gates of understanding to her friend.

They reached the Problem Page. Maria quickly skimmed the columns. "I am twenty-eight, not married, but not a virgin." "Over the years my husband has made me lose all my women friends by making passes at them." "I'd always hoped to marry, but decided to build a career first. I am now forty-two and scared of a lonely old age." Perhaps Sumitra's parents were right to want to protect the girl from becoming a letter on page 61, Maria thought. What must they think of her, a divorced woman with a four-year-old child, until recently living in poverty, disowned by her family, working as a general aide in a hospital and always worrying, until her remarriage, about making ends meet? She knew Mai liked her; she often said that Maria cheered her up, although she couldn't understand much of what she said. But to some extent, the Problem Page represented Maria's society, Maria's life, and this was as alien and as horrific to Mrs. Patel as arranged marriages were to Maria.

She closed the magazine and shrugged. "This is no good. Let's try the book I bought you." The book was quite helpful, starting off with colloquial phrases: "How are you?" "I am well, thank you," but Mai knew these already. Lesson 2 gave useful phrases for visiting a football ground and an ice rink, and Lessons 3 and 4 were about tools and building sites. They both learned about bits and braces, mechanical shovels and hydraulic cranes. "I think you'd better pick it up by just talking to me," Maria sighed. The book was quite useless for Mai, who didn't go skating, wasn't interested in football and had no intention of learning how to build houses. "Pick it up? Pick up the book?" Another explanation was called for.

Now Maria used her hourly lessons for conversation, talking to Mai, making her answer not just by saying yes or no, but developing her thoughts. She didn't feel very competent as a teacher and could find no book that was of any use to someone who had grasped the rudiments of the language but was not interested in technical skills. At least she was becoming more friendly with Mai. Although Maria understood Sumitra's difficulties, she could sympathize, too, with the mother. She saw that Mai was trapped in her past, in her traditional ways of thought, while Sumitra represented a new pattern, one that had not existed before. She couldn't say to Mai, "Well you must accept it, you are living in a different country now, a different society." Mai's idea of that society was page 61. But like the pictures of the glamorous film stars, page 61 represented only a fraction of true British life.

If only Maria could make Mai understand this, if only she could talk to her in words she could comprehend.

CHAPTER XVI

"I'm sorry you've decided to leave," Mr. Jones was saying. A fly buzzed against the window, trying to get out of the room, then flew in circles round the central light before attempting to escape from the stuffy study again. The headmaster's phrases spun round in Sumitra's head as she willed the stupid fly out of the open pane: "Good pupil." "Overcome initial difficulties." "Future prospects." . . . And then the fly was out in the heat of the afternoon. "Let us know how you get on," Mr. Jones told her as he shook her hand, but his eyes were already distant, already focused on the next student coming in through the door. As Sumitra left, she heard the headmaster saying to Robert, "I'm sorry you've decided to leave. . . ."

The school was almost deserted. Only the pupils who were leaving remained to have their statutory chat with Mr. Jones. Apart from the whistling of the caretaker, the buildings were silent. I've passed six years of my life at Northfields, she thought. And I've changed so much. But the school is still the same.

The hot July sun burned down on the pavement, and when the bus finally dawdled up the road, it was practically empty. Everyone seemed to have wilted in the unusual heat; the roads were almost free of traffic and there were few pedestrians. A sense of anticlimax hung in the air as if London itself had begun its summer holiday.

I'm a school leaver, Sumitra told herself as she sat on the upper deck, waiting for a sense of occasion to hit her. But nothing happened. In a way it was like having a birthday, and feeling the same as on the day before. Apart from a pressing need to find a permanent job before Bap arranged for her to work in Jayant's shop, she felt a great hollowness. For the rest of her friends—Hilary, Lynne, Mary, Robert—leaving school heralded the entry into an adult world where they would be expected to make their own decisions, if not at work, then at least at home. They would go out with their friends, pursue their interests and hobbies, begin to carve out their own lives and careers. For her, however, nothing would change. Despite its restrictions, school had been one of the few places where she had been relatively free.

Luckily, Jayant was too involved in arranging the visit of Sri Mahatma Mahavir to the temple to worry about the immediate employment of his reprobate niece. So on the following Monday Sumitra looked in the window of the Goldspear Agency in Muswell Hill Broadway. Lots of jobs were advertised in clear black print. MUSIC DIRECTOR'S SEC. 9-5 £5000. GIRL

FRIDAY REQUIRED IN SHOW BUS. OFFICE. £8000 P.A. MEET THE STARS. IMPRESARIO NEEDS ELEGANT P.A. NO TYPING! Underneath the list of fascinating jobs was the message in scarlet: ENQUIRE WITHIN. NO FEES TO STAFF.

Sumitra glanced at her reflection in the window. She had combed her hair into a secretarial bun and was wearing a dark suit. I don't look too bad, she told herself, then saw that the girl inside the office was staring curiously at her. Sumitra pushed open the heavy door and entered.

"Can I help you?" the clerk asked immediately, her fingers already holding out a registration form.

"I'm looking for a permanent job. I saw one advertised in the window for a music director's secretary." She might get to New York yet!

The clerk was devastated. "Oh, I'm so sorry, that job has just gone, only this morning. I haven't had time to take the notice down yet. But if you fill in these forms," and she waved the papers in her hand beguilingly up and down, "I'm sure we can find you just what you need." Her smile was charming and full of warmth, as if her sole purpose of existence were to ensure that Sumitra got the job she deserved. Sumitra smiled back, then remembered Maria's words of advice. "Don't be taken in by agencies," her friend had told her. "They're O.K. up to a point, but all they're really interested in is their commission."

"I don't want to register unless you've got any jobs."

"Fill in the form first and then I'll have a look," the woman promised.

"But have you any permanent jobs?" Sumitra insisted. "I really am looking seriously."

"Dear"—the clerk's voice was growing icy now—"I can't help you unless you fill in the form. It's one of the rules."

Sumitra gave in, filled out the form and handed it back.

The clerk scanned through it hastily. "Age: seventeen, four

O's and you're going to study for two A's at night school, typing forty, shorthand eighty-five. Not very fast, but you'll pick it up soon, I expect. Can you do switch?"

"Switch?" Sumitra repeated.

"Yes, switchboard, can you operate a switchboard?"

"Oh, yes," said Sumitra. "I've worked one for some years at my Saturday job."

"Well, dear, we haven't any permanent jobs at the moment, I'm afraid, but if you're interest in temping, I can help you."

"Yes, that's O.K." Anything would be better than sitting around at home with Dadima.

The clerk flicked through a card index file. "Here's a job that will suit you down to the ground," she chortled joyously. "There's a vacancy at Remus Ribbons in Highgate; they need someone for four months while the permanent secretary is on holiday. Isn't that super?" The interviewer looked so overcome with delight that anyone would have thought that Sumitra had found *her* a job. Sumitra smiled politely. She didn't know what to say, whether the job would suit her or not, what the job entailed.

The interviewer was already dialing a number. "Hello, Remus Ribbons? Oh, Mr. Remus, have you filled your vacancy for a temp sec yet? This is Goldspear Agency at your service. No? Oh, lovely. I have a young, charming girl, a Miss Sumitra Patel. No, no, she's not black. A lovely Pakistani girl," and she shot a conspiratorial, apologetic glance at Sumitra, who squirmed mournfully on her chair. "She is a super typist with excellent shorthand speeds, telex, audio, switch. Shall I send her round?"

"But I can't do audio typing and my speeds aren't" Sumitra tried to interrupt.

The clerk waved her imperiously back to her chair and frowned. "Yes, right, that will be fine. She should be round in about half an hour!" The woman was scribbling out an introduction card as she talked. "Yes, rates as we discussed before, double the salary plus first week's wages."

She put the phone down and beamed beatifically at her latest recruit. Sumitra was reminded of the photograph of a pundit her father had in his bedroom, a man full of holy happiness. "I had to tell a few white lies," the woman laughed, "but once you're there, I'm sure you'll love Mr. Remus and he'll love you. He's such a sweet man. I must be frank, sometimes it's hard to find jobs for—well, you know, I'm sure you understand." Now she was writing out a time sheet. "Here we are, dear." She was all smiles and sympathy now. "We pay seventy pence an hour and you get paid on Friday afternoons. Or you can come in on Saturday for your check, as you only live round the corner. If there are any problems, just let me know, right? Goldspear Agency looks after its girls. Best of luck, dear!"

Remus Ribbons turned out to be a converted warehouse in the back of a private home in Shepherd's Hill. The door was opened by a tiny wizened man who introduced himself as Mr. Remus. "Come in, come in, come in," he barked. "I'm Mr. Remus. This is your office. You will type letters and answer the phone." He had a sandy handlebar moustache that made him look like a fox. Remus the fox, she thought, and wanted to laugh. Sumitra hung her jacket over a chair and looked round the tiny office. There was no switchboard, no telex, so the agency lady had not needed to lie. The typewriter was a prewar model; Sumitra found a piece of scrap paper and practiced *Now is the time for all good men to come to the aid of the party.* Mr. Remus ran in with a pile of scribbled letters and rushed out again. Sumitra hunted for stationery, flimsies, carbon, eraser, and began to type.

By Tuesday she had finished most of the letters and the phone had rung twice. "Trade is slack now," Mr. Remus told her briefly. "Summer is a slack time in the rag trade." He was not a communicative person, but she gathered he bought braidings and bindings from abroad and supplied stores throughout the Home Counties. "You have the rest of this week to learn the ropes, and then I'm off to an exhibition in Rumania. Here." He pulled a crumpled brochure from his pocket. It read, *The People's Republic of Rumania Ribbon and Braiding Exhibition, Bucharest.* "I'll be away for two weeks—we're being shown over factories and design centers, so you'll have to run the office until I get back. I'm sure you'll manage." As if overwhelmed by this long speech, he suddenly turned and dashed out of the office.

Before she went home on Friday night, Mr. Remus entrusted her with the keys. "Don't forget now, you're running the office. Deal with anything that comes up if you can. If it's something difficult, tell them to wait till I return. Goodbye."

"Honestly," she told Maria as they jogged around the park the next day. "Talk about a meteoric rise to fame. One day I'm a school leaver, and the next I'm running a ribbon emporium single-handed!"

"I always said you'd go far," panted Maria, "but I'll get there first." With a sudden spurt, she overtook Sumitra, but soon sank onto the grass. Sumitra flopped down beside her. Maria gasped, her sides heaving with exertion. "I'll have to give up running soon. I'm going to have another baby."

"Maria, how terrific! Congratulations! I bet Martin's pleased."

"Yes, he is, he's over the moon, and Sally's thrilled, too. I never thought she'd have a brother or sister. . . ."

Sumitra picked at the grass. "Everything seems to be working out for you, Maria, doesn't it? Don't think I resent that . . . it's just that at one time your life seemed as muddled and confused as mine, but now you're settled and happy."

"Don't," pleaded Maria. "You make me sound like an old woman. But I must admit I never thought I'd be as happy as I am now. It hasn't always been like that, you know," she added, squeezing Sumitra's hand comfortingly.

"They're talking of sending me away again," confided Sumitra. "You know they were going to send me to India after the pub fiasco. They threatened to lock me up and put me on a plane. I know it sounds incredible, but that's what they're like. And that would have been the end of me. Now they're talking of sending me to my aunt's house in Birmingham. She's got a spare room and I'd go to college there. I don't really care what I do anymore. If I do what I want to, I'll bring disgrace to their name—that's all they care about, their name, not about me. They say the others won't find husbands if I shame the name. So I must do what they want or leave home. I don't want to do either."

It was stiflingly hot. The sun warmed their arms and legs. Maria was reminded of the heat on the day she had left her first husband. "I've told you about when I left Dave, haven't I? I expect it sounds romantic, running off through the vineyards, getting on a plane. But it was a hard decision to make and I knew that when I got back to England I'd get no help from anyone. I didn't know where to go, what to do, and I had a tiny baby dependent on me. I don't talk about those times much, but they were really awful, the worst three years of my life. But I got through them, people do get through bad times, and now I've got a smashing husband, a lovely home, a beautiful daughter and another baby on the way. I've got good friends and Sally is happy. I never thought I'd know contentment like this. You'll find happiness, too, one way or another."

A plane flew overhead, carrying unknown people to unknown destinations. "I don't think the trouble is really anything to do with being Indian or black, or Pakistani, or Greek, or Jewish. I think it's to do with being You. I'm English, my family is English, but because they believe it's the woman's place to follow the husband and obey him, they couldn't accept that I wouldn't do that. They don't want to know what my life was really like, they aren't interested—for them, Dave will always be the innocent victim and I'll be the wicked woman. Sometimes families are like chains that tie you down so they can continue in the same thoughtless stupid way for generations. But some people—and you are one of them—have to go their own way, think their own thoughts."

Sumitra thought about this as she chewed a blade of grass. At school she had seen representatives of various groups—Jews, Greeks, Turks, Arabs, Chinese, West Indians, Irish—all happily playing together and conforming to the larger ideal of the school community, but going home to continue living in the ways of their parents. They went off to Jewish/Greek/Turkish/Irish youth clubs so that they would marry Jewish/Greek/Turkish/Irish children. What was it all for? Why couldn't they all mix with whom they liked and bring their children up as human beings living in a country called England?

"My grandma told Ela and Bimla not to play with white children," she said. "I was really upset. What chance have they got? How can they think their own thoughts?"

"Sumitra, they'll have the same chance as you. I know you see racism from both sides, but it's not only people like your parents and Jayant who will shape them. Sandya and you and Lynne and Martin will influence them, too. They will have to make up their own minds, when they are older."

Another plane flew by. "I still want to be an air hostess," Sumitra said dreamily as she watched it disappear into the distance. "But my dad just won't talk about it."

A group of small boys began to play football on the grass in front of them. A flock of birds that had been nesting on the trees flew away in protest. Ela and Sally dashed up hand in hand and threw themselves on the recumbent figures, squealing and laughing. "I'm hungry, Mummy!" shouted Sally.

"Let's go and find Sandya and buy some ice creams, then," Maria replied.

Before the end of the summer, there were more incidents of racial unrest.

A gang of English youths had attacked some Asian boys. The Asian community of Southall suggested forming a vigilante committee. This was frowned on by those who thought that the police were the right people to deal with incidents of this nature. Every night there were discussions at home as they ate their evening meal. Bap felt that the police were not doing enough; Mai was frightened and would not go out alone. Ela and Bimla stood close together at the bus stop in the evenings. Sandya and Sumitra were anxious and perturbed.

Sumitra had never told anyone about the dream. In the dream, she was waiting at the bus stop one night after work, and the thugs had come upon her from behind. "Paki, Paki!" they screeched as two of them held her arms while the third punched her over and over until her teeth had gone, her eyes were blinded with blood and her ribs kicked and broken. The brave and goodly citizens of Highgate trod over her until, at last, one of them stopped and picked her up. The face of the Good Samaritan was black. Just before she died, she recognized who it was. It was Yusuf, the houseboy.

Sumitra and Sandya started to listen to the phone-in programs. The race issue was discussed almost every evening for several months. The callers seemed to fall into certain categories. There were the Some-of-my-best-friends type of calls, which went: "Some of my best friends are black: I don't want you to think I'm prejudiced, but the other day I saw a West Indian woman push a white lady out of the way at the bus stop." There were the They've-taken-our-jobs brigade: "They come over here, black, brown, yellow, take our jobs and our houses, fill the streets with the smell of their cooking. . . ."

Then there was the Live-and-let-live party: "I don't mind immigrants, Nigel. I think it makes life more interesting." There was also the occasional immigrant complaining of discrimination, or, more rarely, stating that no hostility existed.

The presenters were more uniform. Sumitra noticed that a person calling from the National Front was either cut off immediately or allowed three seconds in which to express a view. She made Sandya stand, watch at the ready, timing each call. The phone-in announcers presented the white liberal attitude, usually recommending unlimited immigration and scolding callers who did not agree for being prejudiced. "They don't seem to know that there's a race problem in this country," Sumitra said. "They seem to think everything's great, that everybody loves their neighbors."

Sandya sighed. "Hmm. I wonder where they live, these announcers, or what schools their kids go to? I wonder if they really ever talk to anyone—I mean really hear what other people are saying?"

"Sometimes," confided Sumitra, "I imagine that they don't really exist. They may just be great big mouths, robots, without any ears to hear with—monsters, who can only talk."

It seemed to be true. The presenters hissed and snapped at anyone who did not say what they wanted to hear, cutting callers off and then adding a sarcastic comment from within their soundproofed safety. Freedom of speech, thought Sumitra, should be two-way. It could be dangerous to deny people with genuine grievances access to what they felt was the only channel where they could publicly state their beliefs.

Sumitra and Sandya listened to these conversations with amusement and horror. "Do you think there should be unlimited immigration?" asked Sandya.

"I don't think so," Sumitra told her. "Britain's a small country, it's hard enough for those of us here to integrate, let alone allowing more and more people to come in. If we were adapting better, it probably wouldn't matter, but we aren't really accepted as a group, and goodness knows we see enough of Mai's generation who don't even *want* to be accepted!"

Mai and Bap still discussed getting a shop. They had even begun to go off at weekends looking at vacant premises. None of these was ever actually followed up—they were always too expensive, or too far away, or too dilapidated—but the search itself gave reality to their dreams. This was another thing that the callers complained of. A hardworking, diligent community had moved into a lazy and apathetic society, tired by two major wars, saddled with a class system, dulled by responsibilities, financial worries and too much rain. A grave vitamin D deficiency seemed to have sapped the nation's strength. A vigorous, bright group of people had arrived, willing to work hours that the natives did not want to work, buying shops the natives did not wish to own, providing a service the natives did not want to provide. So they phoned up, these natives, saying that another corner shop had fallen, another post office had been invaded. As the autumn nights drew in, the calls became less, dwindled and finally stopped. Outwardly, things went on as before.

Mr. Remus had returned from Rumania, bringing Sumitra some sample lengths of handwoven ribbon with a folklore motif. The office had not burned down, there had been no disasters, and the rest of her stay there was a calm and happy one. On her final day, he ceremoniously presented her with a huge reel of braid from the warehouse. Sumitra gave it to Mai to hem round the edge of her new sari.

Sumitra had her name down with the Job Centre, as well as at the Goldspear Agency. During her final week at Remus Ribbons, the Job Centre had contacted her about an interesting vacancy on their books. This was in a detective agency, and Sumitra agreed to go for an interview. She dressed carefully, waiting till all her sisters had gone to school. She bathed, dusted herself with the talc Hilary had given her for Christmas, and put on her black suit with a crisply ironed white blouse and her highest heels. Brushing her hair, she swept it back into a snood. The mirror reflected a tall, slim girl dressed in the latest fashion with arresting features and beautiful eyes. She collected several wolf whistles as she walked to the bus.

A detective agency sounded interesting. Stories of espionage, drugs, high finance ran through her head. She imagined Mr. Farley to be a cross between Shashi Kabur and Errol Flynn and was slightly disappointed when a plump, balding man shook her hand and ushered her into a seat.

"First I'll tell you a bit about the job," said Mr. Farley. "I expect you think it's very exciting, but in fact it's mainly routine: missing persons, correspondents in divorce cases, petty swindles. Occasionally something out of the ordinary comes up, but that's only about twice a year."

The door opened and a young woman came in, carrying two cups of coffee. "This is Pamela. She's going to America soon." Pamela grinned at Sumitra and left the room. They heard her typewriter clicking in the outer office.

"There's one thing that's bothering me about employing you." Mr. Farley picked up his coffee and took a precise sip from the cup. "You have four O-levels and I see you're taking two A-levels at night school. I think you may be overqualified for this work. It's basically straightforward typing, very simple office work, and I feel you might soon get bored. I do like my secretaries to stay for some time. Pamela's been with me for five years, since she left school. As a private detective, I have a certain amount of intuition about people. You don't really want to be a secretary, do you? You wouldn't stay here long?"

Sumitra sighed. For the last few years, teachers had been telling her to work hard, to study, to pass exams or else she wouldn't get a job. She had worked, sandwiching her studies in with all her other duties, and now this man was telling her she had worked too hard, that she was overqualified! "I don't know what to say," she muttered, staring out of the window.

Why was it called Green Street? There were hardly any trees.

"What do you really want to do?" asked Mr. Farley.

Sumitra suddenly decided to tell him. It wouldn't make any difference now; he wasn't going to employ her anyway. "I want to be an air hostess," she said, "but I can't go on a training course till I'm twenty-one."

"I'm glad you've been truthful," he said. "I'm sure you understand my concern. I think you'd be better off in something connected with the hotel trade, or the travel business, where you'd get experience in the sort of skills you'll require. I have a suggestion to make. Come and work here till I find a permanent replacement for Pamela or until you find permanent employment for yourself. I'll let you have time off to look for other positions and I'll pay you temporary rates." He mentioned sixty pounds plus luncheon vouchers. Nearly double the Goldspear rates! Sumitra was delighted. "Can you start on Monday?"

She left his office feeling happy and free. She had a job to go to on Monday and it was Guy Fawkes Night. Maria and Martin were coming round that evening to build a fire. "I've got a job!" she told Sandya excitedly as she got home.

"Great!" said Sandya, smiling. It wasn't often that Sumitra seemed happy anymore.

Martin arrived and began stacking twigs and wooden scraps for the fire. Bap had a broken chair to sacrifice. The children played in the frosty air, screaming with delight as the flames caught hold, leaping higher and higher into the sky. Bap and Mai came into the garden, eyes glowing in the firelight. The smoke from their fire rose up, mingling with the smoke from other fires in the neighborhood.

Bap looked at the collection of fireworks in the flickering light. He had almost forgotten the pleasure of a fireworks display. He turned them over, muttering the names to himself. "Catherine Wheel, sparklers, Golden Joy, Silver Spray." He felt the old joy rekindle. At least in this strange and cold land there were fireworks! Sally crept up beside him and put her hand in his. She was awed by the crackling bonfire and the sudden whooshes and whizzes from nearby gardens. He smiled down at her and gave her a sparkler, laughing at the child's astonishment as it fizzled and spat golden droplets into the sky.

"Let me have one, Bap!"

"And me!" implored Ela and Bimla.

Soon they were all holding sparklers while Bap let off the rest of the fireworks. The children clapped and cheered after each bang.

Maria fed potatoes into the flames, testing them with a wooden spike and passing them around. Martin retrieved chestnuts and Mai brought out mugs of coffee, and they ate and drank, shivering in the cold air, while the sky was a riot of orange and gold. Sumitra looked down at her hand, remembering the time she'd been burned by the firework at Leela's wedding. The scar was still there, just visible beneath the brown smooth skin.

CHAPTER XVII

It was several weeks before she stumbled on the case of Varsha Nahri. Sumitra was tidying up the filing cabinet and came upon the Missing Persons section. The name leaped out at her, startling among the Jennings and Hutchinsons and Browns. At lunchtime, instead of window-shopping in Oxford Street or meeting a friend for coffee, she opened the file and sat down to read.

The correspondence inside the file related to a young Indian girl who had left home. Her parents had contacted the agency in the hope of finding their daughter. Mr. Farley had agreed to handle the case on one condition: that he would not divulge the girl's address if he managed to trace her. He would find out if she was safe, ask her to contact her parents, but that was all.

At the back of the file were some clips sent in by a cuttings service, detailing a few suicide cases. All the names were of Asian girls who had killed themselves. One of the coroner's reports said, "I dread making out even one more report on a pathetic little girl found floating in a river."

Sumitra read through the case history of this unknown stranger who suddenly seemed to represent her own dilemma. Varsha, twenty-one years old, had been found living in Ealing in a bed-sitter. Mr. Farley had spoken to her; Varsha said that she had to leave home—her parents were insisting that she marry an accountant of their acquaintance while she had no desire to do so. She was studying at London University and wanted to complete her studies and have a career before even thinking about getting married.

She agreed to write to her parents regularly, to phone them occasionally, but not to see them, explaining that they would try to pressure her into returning home, where once again she would be subject to family demands to conform to a way of life she did not want to lead. They had, she said, beaten her, locked her in her room and threatened to send her to India if she continued to act as she was doing.

Sumitra lit a cigarette. Her hand was shaking. She had heard of Indian girls leaving home, but had never met anyone who had actually done so. Those girls who had run away were talked about in tones of envy by those of her own age, and in hushed voices of disgust and shame by her parents' generation. But as far as she knew, no one had ever come into contact with anyone who had left home without their parents' consent.

All her Indian friends discussed leaving home. It was like her parents' wish to own a shop, or the neighbors' longing for a cottage by the sea. It was a myth, a legend to cling to, an empty dream that would never come true, but which was comforting and consoling. One of her friends, Sulima, had often spoken of going away, of finding a flat, and had even got as far as looking in the Accommodations Vacant columns in the papers. But both Sulima and Sumitra knew that she would not leave. It was as if expressing the wish were enough, it defined hopes and needs, but putting the wish into effect would break her mother's heart, disgrace her family, mar her brothers' and sisters' chances of marrying well, bring the family name into disrepute with the rest of the Indian community. Sumitra listened to her, expressed the same desire, and hung back for the same reasons.

She read through the file again and frowned. If she did leave home—and her heart missed a beat at the thought—*if* she left home, how would the family react? Mai and Bap would be devastated. They both relied on her so much, they would never manage without her. But then again, if she married soon, as they wanted her to, they would have to cope without her anyway. This was not really the issue.

She thought about the burden it would throw on Sandya. Sandya would have to manage alone. She seemed so thin and vulnerable, yet in so many ways she had turned out to be stronger, more determined than Sumitra. Sandya would manage; that was not the real stumbling block either.

The crucial point was Sumitra, whether she herself possessed enough courage to leave home. She wasn't sure that she did. It was true that other boys and girls of her own age, even younger, set up homes every day on their own, but it was one thing to be independent with the approval and encouragement of a family, and another to do something that meant cutting herself off forever from the whole way of life and the people she loved.

She needed to talk to someone outside the situation, someone understanding and sympathetic. She phoned home and told Mai that she was going to visit Maria after work. Mai agreed, but told her to be home by eight o'clock as some visitors were coming.

Later that day, Sumitra joined the commuters streaming into Marble Arch station. Her mind raced as she swayed in the crowded carriage. Looking round at the people packed like battery hens in a cage, she caught the eye of an Indian girl squashed up against the doorway. Is that Varsha Nahri? Sumitra wondered. And if it isn't, would she like to be? She stared at all the passengers in turn, black, white, brown, Mediterranean. They were crushed together so closely that they seemed to be locked in a hideous embrace, but they would never know each other's name, or occupation, or hopes and fears. The faces were like labels—black male aged thirty, white female aged twenty-two—but behind and beneath the labels were hidden secrets.

She shifted her bag from one hand to the other, noticing that the leather strap had made a dark indentation in her skin. Camden Town. The train half-emptied, passengers pushing off, stumbling, stretching cramped limbs. Another wave of commuters struggled on, shoving to find seats, complaining about the long wait, then silently retiring into themselves. The train moved off. Day after day, it went back and forth like a monstrous man-eating snake, never changing, never varying. Only the faces changed. As they drew into Highgate station, she noticed a poster advertising a film at the Everyman Cinema. The film was called *Dante's Inferno*. She grinned wryly. That was the ultimate irony, advertising the inferno while they were being consumed by it.

Maria was giving Sally her tea when Sumitra arrived. "Hello, Sumitra, what a lovely surprise!" Sumitra was swept into the house, seated at the table and given a mug of coffee and a plate of biscuits.

"Hello, Mitra," beamed Sally. "I've got new shoes." She stuck out her feet.

"They're lovely!" Sumitra admired them.

"I've got new socks, too!" Sally pulled off her new shoes to show a pair of grubby white socks. "And"—the child paused dramatically to gain maximum effect for her *pièce de résistance*—"I've got new knickers, too!" Sally jumped off her chair and pulled up her dress.

"Very pretty," Sumitra agreed. "They've got chickens, and cats and dogs on them."

"Finish your tea now, and go out to play," Maria told her. "Sumitra's tired."

Sally sneaked a biscuit off Sumitra's plate and ran out, chuckling.

Maria's waist was thickening. Once she had the new baby to look after, Sumitra would feel even more excluded and out of place. Although Maria and Martin always told her she was welcome, she knew they had their own lives to lead, a young family to bring up. At the guesthouse, they had all been preoccupied, on their own. Maria would always be her friend, she knew that, but Maria's life was now so full, so busy. It wasn't fair to intrude.

"What's the matter, love?" Maria asked kindly. "What's wrong? Are you in trouble again at home?"

"No, it's nothing in particular. It's just that this afternoon I found a file in the office and I read it. It was about this Indian girl who left home and her parents asked Mr. Farley to trace her. It really set me thinking, but I don't know what to do. Oh, Maria, everything seems so hopeless. I've got to decide soon. If I stay at home, I'll have to accept my parents' laws, their customs, their traditions. I don't think I can do that. I don't only want to mix with Indian people—I don't think about people like that. My heart isn't brown—do you know what I mean? If I like someone, I want to be their friend, no matter what culture they come from; and if I don't like them, I just want to ignore them, even if they are Indian. I can't get married to someone I don't really know—I've become too English to do that. I don't think I want to get married at all. And I need time to learn, to think, to experiment." She wiped her eyes, sighing heavily as she did so.

"Sumitra, don't get upset. I'll make some more coffee and some sandwiches. Martin's staying late at school tonight so I wasn't going to bother with a proper meal."

"Maria, you never cook proper meals!" The joke surprised her, she didn't feel like laughing, but just being with Maria seemed to calm her down. As Maria bustled about, Sumitra looked around the kitchen. Every windowsill, every available inch of space, was taken up by another of Maria's hobbies. Sumitra had never known anyone to try so many things. There were hand-embroidered lavender doilies, painted tiles, brightly lacquered wooden pots and spoons, and homemade candles. From the towel rack hung a mandolin, and a tin whistle lay on top of the fridge. There was a guitar in the broom cupboard and an accordion in the vegetable box.

Sumitra sighed again. She wanted, needed, time to grow, to search, to experiment, fail, succeed. She rested her head on her hands, feeling the tears pricking her lids. "If only we hadn't left Uganda, or if only we'd gone to India, I wouldn't have known any other life. I wouldn't be so confused and unhappy. I'd just have done what everyone else did, not questioning, not worrying about it. I feel so tense and hung up. I guess I have for weeks and weeks without realizing it, and now I've just read about someone who has actually done what I think I must do. But should I make the break? Am I being selfish, doing something that will upset the whole family, ruin my sisters' chance of marriage? Five people's lives will be spoiled to make one person happy." She glanced at Maria through wet lashes. "What shall I do?"

Maria set sandwiches and coffee on the table. Looking at Sumitra, she saw a beautiful young woman pulled in two directions, felt Sumitra's inner strength and drive. Within her own body, a new life was growing, to be born into a world that could be cruel and savage, as well as loving and kind.

"I can't tell you what to do, Sumitra. I'm hardly in a position to hand out advice myself, and, anyway, I'm your mum's friend as well as yours. I won't tell you what to do, but I think you know what I'd do if I were in your position."

Sumitra picked a crumb off the table. "You'd go, wouldn't you?"

Maria nodded. Pushing her dark hair from her forehead, she said, "It's very hard when you don't want to hurt people, but sometimes it seems as if it's the only way. You know the score, you know what will happen if you stay at home. Your parents will be happy, but you won't. You'll be trapped on the conveyor belt and carried off into 'the great sausage machine.' "

"Yes, yes!" Sumitra cried excitedly, getting up from the table and walking around the kitchen, unable to contain her thoughts by sitting down. "That's just it, Maria! You call it the sausage machine, I call it the Banquo line. But it's the same thing. It means doing something because it's always been done, even if you don't want to do it, even if you think it's wrong, because not continuing the tradition will cause too much trouble. So you get a long line of conformists doing what is expected of them. That's fair enough when the expectations are reasonable and rational, but when they lead to fear and isolation and hatred and . . ." Her voice broke and she sat down.

Maria clapped her hands. "More, more!" she applauded. "You'll be prime minister if you carry on like that." Then she added more soberly, "In your place, I would leave home. There really is no other way. Otherwise you'll become like Sulima and your other friends. Sulima won't leave home, although she never talks about anything else. I don't think she's brave enough. She can't help it, that's how she is. But you, you are brave enough. There's something different about you, I've always felt that. You know it will be hard, perhaps being outcast from your family, but you must decide if you can take that, and, if you can, do what you must. You know you can count on your friends; Martin and I will always support you, and you've got your friends from Hanbury's and your schoolmates. Sometimes friends are more important than family. I've learned that!"

She took the plates off the table and began to wash up. "One thing, though, if you do decide to go, be very careful. I don't know what your family might do—they may really pack you off to India this time. So make sure you keep it a secret."

Sally ran back into the house. "Mark called me a pig, so I punched him and he's gone to tell his mummy," she related excitedly.

Maria gave Sumitra a weary smile as she cuddled her daughter. "You think you've got problems—see what fascinating lives we lead!"

Sally dived into the fridge and emerged with a chunk of cheese and a packet of cards. "I wondered where those were!" said Maria.

"Mitra, will you play Happy Families with us?" demanded Sally.

Maria grinned. "She's not very tactful, is she?"

"No, she's not!" agreed Sumitra, throwing the plump little girl into the air and catching her as Sally screamed with delight. "O.K., let's play Happy Families. Why not!"

"You're late," Mai scolded as she came in at quarter past eight.

"Your mother has been worried about you, girl," chided Dadima. "You should be more considerate to her. You should not go out alone at night, anyway."

Sumitra fought down the impulse to shout and swear, and smiled instead. "Don't worry, Dadima," she said. "In India it gets dark very early, that's why girls aren't allowed out alone at night. But look outside, it's still quite light."

She went to help Mai prepare the food. Nagin and some other friends were coming to visit and potatoes for the *Alu Chachari* had to be peeled. Sandya had been conscripted into making *roti.* Her black hair was smudged with flour and she smelled of *ghee.*

When the guests arrived, Sumitra was surprised to see that Kirit from the washing-machine warehouse was among them. As she and Sandya took in the food, he gave her a long, searching look. Sumitra was aware that the scene had a certain charm. Nagin had brought his sitar and his brother. The brother had brought a tabla, and they were seated on the floor, improvising a rhythmic tune while the men clapped their hands, fingertips to palm, and the wives, relegated to another room, helped prepare the meal, tapping their feet as they worked. Dadima was seated in her special chair, her white sari tucked loosely around her, one bare foot splayed on the floor before her while she sat cheerfully balancing on the other and deftly rolling cotton-wool balls between gnarled fingers to make candles for the *puja.*

If only I could paint, thought Sumitra. The group was like an exotic subject for a Van Gogh or Rubens masterpiece. She wished she could capture the rich colors of the saris, the gleam of the silver dishes with *Made in India* stamped on their undersides, laden now with rice and *paratas* and spiced potatoes.

She could marry Kirit and be part of the picture, part of the bright scene. She would then have status in the community, an allotted place, a defined role. Everything would be so easy; there would be no problems to solve, no worries to threaten her. But—and she still was not sure, was not certain—was this the right way for her? Did she belong in that picture? Did she belong in any picture anywhere?

Kirit looked handsome and pleasant, but she would never be left alone with him or know what he was like until after they were married. She wondered savagely if Mrs. Baker, so keen on minority groups retaining their customs, would want Lynne to be forced into an arranged marriage at the age of eighteen, or if she only wanted others to practice their foreign ways in order to make her own life appear more colorful.

Sumitra felt like a caterpillar whose skin had grown too tight but was not yet ready to take a step into the unknown. The chrysalis was safe and warm.

CHAPTER XVIII

Although the Goldspear Agency still had glossy jobs advertised in the window, they seemed to have forgotten that Sumitra's name was on their books. But the Job Centre phoned her up at work with news of a permanent position. "It's in a travel agency," explained the clerk. "They want someone to do shorthand typing, counter work and bookings. It sounds like what you wanted, doesn't it?"

Sumitra's voice was suddenly tight and dry. She managed to squeak a reply and took down the address the girl dictated. Waiting until her heart had returned to its normal seventy-two beats per minute, she phoned to make an appointment. Then she went to tell Mr. Farley. He smiled and wished her luck. "Of course you can go. I'm sure you'll get the job, and if they want you to start on Monday, that's all right."

Thursday afternoon was bright and clear. As she entered the swing doors of the agency, she felt an aura of confidence spreading brightly around her. "Don't forget," Mr. Farley had advised. "Sell yourself. Don't concentrate on what you can't do, emphasize what you *can* do!" A counter clerk showed her into a back waiting room and a secretary soon arrived to take her to the manager's office.

A small, plump man rose beaming from behind a desk. "Miss Patel, I am delighted to meet you. I am Mr. de Souza. I have good reports from the Job Centre of how you are getting on in your present employment. Please sit down." He indicated a chair. Sumitra sank into one of the red plastic armchairs, noticing Mr. de Souza's strong Portuguese accent and aware of the power and energy flowing from his body.

A look of extreme misery passed over his expressive face. Sumitra wondered if he was in pain. "Dear Miss Patel," he apologized. "I am so sorry, but I am afraid I must test your abilities." She stared at him, bewildered. "Take a letter." He breathed deeply and began dictating: "Dear Sir, with reference to . . ." Sumitra looked around for something to write on, suddenly realizing what he meant. Should she stop him in full flow? She suppressed a strong desire to laugh, and then Mr. de Souza noticed that she was sitting motionless in the chair and chuckled.

"I am so stupid! Please forgive me, my dear. Here is a piece of paper and a pencil."

He began again at an incredible speed, pronouncing the foreign words with panache. "Dear Sir, with reference to your letter of the eighteenth inst., I regret that we are unable to accommodate you in the Italia Hotel, Milan, for the dates you require." Without a pause, he continued: "This is a typical problem, a typical problem you will have to deal with, should you get the job." As her pencil flew over the paper, Sumitra realized that he was no longer dictating to her, and crossed out the last sentence. Just as she had relaxed her grip on the pencil, he was off again, and she wildly chased his words across the line. "We can arrange for you to stay at the Adelphi Hotel, which is equal in quality and not far from the Italia, for the same dates." Sumitra managed to keep up with him, thankful that her shorthand skill had improved in the time spent at the detective agency. She was ushered into a smaller office and left to type out the letter.

Mr. de Souza was ecstatic about the result. "Good, good! Excellent, excellent! Do you know, Miss Patel, the last girl I interviewed couldn't even spell ship? Can you imagine that, coming to work at a travel agency without being able to spell ship! Ridiculous! This is good, good!"

He pulled a huge tin of snuff out of his pocket and offered it to Sumitra. "You would like?"

"No, thanks," Sumitra replied.

He rolled the tobacco between his fingers and inserted it into his flaring nostrils. Then he took a large yellow handkerchief from his other pocket and blew his nose violently.

"Now I tell about job. Seventy pounds a week. This is good for a girl of your age. You see, my dear Miss Patel, I pay good wages for good workings. First a month trial period. Then if we like you and you like us, I give you eighty pounds a week!" Sumitra tried not to gasp. That was incredible, even more than Bap earned. "Hours nine to five-thirty. Saturdays one morning in four. You will work in the office and relieve as counter and booking clerk. Here are prospects, there is much chance of promotion. And with your Russian O-level . . ."

Before leaving the office, she was shown photographs of Mr. de Souza's wife, children and grandchildren, and his home in Oporto. Then he took her round and introduced her to her future colleagues. In a daze, she smiled at the booking clerks and Mr. de Souza's assistant.

Once outside in the street, she grinned at a passing road sweeper. At last she had found a permanent job when she had almost despaired of getting one. Some of her friends were still unemployed and she knew that often she would not even have been granted an interview because of her name. Some employers, despite the Commission for Racial Equality, would not consider taking on a Patel, an Asian, a foreigner. That was part of the problem—while she wanted to leave the encircling culture of her parents, there were other forces eager to push her back inside it. Sometimes she feared that between them these conflicts would squash her, leaving her dry and spent until she became like an autumn leaf driven by the wind with no power or will of its own. Getting a steady job was the first step in putting a foot outside the circle.

Walking down the road, trying to appear mature and sophisticated, she was mentally laughing and turning cartwheels in her mind. Mr. de Souza appeared an incredible character, so full of life and warmth and funny habits. She couldn't remember now which name fitted which face. Was Maureen the pretty black girl, or was that Ava? Was Mr. de Souza's assistant called Gwynneth or Maureen? She couldn't wait until Monday to find out.

Now she could begin to plan. She told no one at home about her new job. She didn't want her parents to be able to contact her at work. They assumed that she was still working for Mr. Farley.

Her days were soon divided between clerical and counter work. The Lisbonia Agency booked flights and arranged journeys all over the world, but specialized in Spanish, Portuguese and Eastern European tours. There was so much to learn. Counter procedure, bookings, reservations, cancellations, dockets, emergency procedures, currency conversions. It was a whole new world, exciting and mysterious. Every time the door opened and someone came over to her, the client was putting his trust in her. It might be a wealthy person to whom a flight to Mustique was as ordinary as a 263 bus ride was to her, or a grandmother spending her life savings on a trip to see her family in America. Sumitra had to be careful, disciplined, responsible. For the first few weeks, she had no time to worry about anything other than trying to master her new duties.

It was fascinating and wearing—the challenge she needed. At night she arrived home too late to help with the housework, and after walking from the station flopped exhausted into bed. Exhilarated by the new work, she found that home problems were in abeyance, even nonexistent. Because she was happy at work, the domestic situation seemed less bleak, and she was too tired to want to go out, glad of the chance to rest at home.

The best thing about the job was that it had prospects. If she still wanted to be an air hostess in three years' time, she could go into a training course without spending the next few years working as ground staff. It would help her gain an entry into the airlines, or if she continued working at the Lisbonia, there were all sorts of possibilities—courier work, overseas inspections, an entrée into a glamorous, exciting world. Sumitra felt pulled by the need to do something greater than leading a humdrum life rearing humdrum children.

It was enjoyable, too, after months of working in lonely offices, to meet and mix with a crowd of young workmates. At lunchtimes they went to the local park or to the pub, laughing and joking about the morning's clients, or Mr. de Souza's dictation, or a booking error. They talked about their plans, their families, their homes. Maureen was getting married soon and intended to get pregnant as soon as possible so that she could stay at home. Ava was studying French and German at night school—she wanted to work abroad for a few years. "You're so lucky!" she told Sumitra. "You can speak French, Russian, Gujarati, Hindi and English. I bet you could get a job anywhere!"

For her eighteenth birthday, Martin and Maria gave her a transistor radio. Bap began searching once more for a shop, taking Mai on weekend trips to Wolverton, Surbiton, Leicester. They always returned with the same tales—too far, too much, too decrepit—but one day they would return with news of success. Then she would have to leave her job to help run the shop. At least now she had the days to look forward to, but when Ava got a spare ticket for a concert, or Maureen invited her to a party, Sumitra had to refuse. She was not allowed to stay out late or go out alone, except to work.

She looked at the transistor radio. If she left home, she would need a radio; maybe that was why Maria had given it to her. It was a symbol of independence. Sumitra began to think about where she would go if she did leave home. Her parents had many acquaintances all over North London, so she would have to find a place south of the river. But what sort of place would it be? A bed-sitter would be too lonely; much as she longed for peace and time alone, she did not want the total isolation of a lodging room. She began to have doubts again, to think of resigning herself to her fate and the uncle's son. At least that would be useful if the washing machine broke down again!

It was Maureen who told her. She was doing her hair with an Afro comb in the cloakroom, teasing the curls into a wide frame round her attractive face, when Sumitra had come in and grinned at her in the mirror. "Hey, Sue," Maureen greeted her. "Did you know that Gwynneth's looking for a new flat-mate?"

Gwynneth worked in one of the adjoining rooms leading off Mr. de Souza's office. It was her job as assistant manager to arrange itineraries and tours for the more adventurous traveler. Her desk and walls were covered with maps and drawings of Russia, America, China, Iceland and Africa. Sumitra knocked on the door and as she went in she heard Gwynneth muttering Russian names to herself while calculating distances on a calculator and marking them onto a three-dimensional map.

"Hello, Sue, Tobolsk, Sverdlovsk, Leningrad." She reached out and took a large green felt-tipped pen from the array of markers in front of her.

"Gwynneth," Sumitra said excitedly, "Maureen's just told me about the flat. Can I talk to you about it?"

Gwynneth looked surprised. "Are you looking for somewhere to live? I had no idea. Look, Sue, I'm really busy at the moment. I've got to finish this itinerary by eleven o'clock. Let's have lunch at the Blue Boy and talk about it then."

At lunchtime they got a table in the crowded pub. As they ate a plowman's lunch, Gwynneth told Sumitra about the flat. "It's in Richmond, not far from the park. There are four bedrooms. I have one, then there's Ben, who's an art student. Jenny's a doctor, and Betsy's a lab technician. They both work at the local hospital, but Betsy's going to Canada soon. We need someone to take her place."

Sumitra stared into her orange juice, twisting the glass around in her fingers till the liquid splashed onto the beer mat. "Would you consider me moving in?" she asked.

"Why on earth not?" said Gwynneth heartily. "You could teach me Russian. I've been meaning to learn it for years. That would help enormously in my job. I would have offered you the room, but I had no idea that you wanted to leave home."

"I don't really want to, that's the trouble, it's so hard to explain."

"Don't think I can't understand," smiled Gwynneth. "I know what you mean. It was the same for me in a way. I come from Gwalchmai, a little village in North Wales. My parents are conventional, chapel-going folk, and I knew by the time I was four that that life wasn't for me. They didn't want me to leave—think London is the City of Sin, they do—but I argued and persuaded, and here I am! They don't know I'm in a mixed flat, of course. Wouldn't do to tell them the uncensored truth, but they do know I'm happy, with an interesting job and good friends."

"It's not only my parents," insisted Sumitra, wondering if Gwynneth really did understand. "You see, it's my sisters, too. There are three of them. My parents would never allow me to leave home, which means that if I do leave I'll have to run away—and I might ruin my sisters' lives by doing so. You don't know what some Indian parents are like. My sisters may never marry because I've disgraced the family name."

"Marry!" laughed Gwynneth. "What would they want to marry for? If their future husbands are so fussy, they're better off unmarried. That's ridiculous. No, love, you do what you want to. Anyway, you never know what will happen. You may stay at home all docile and obedient and then find that your sisters run off and you'll be the one left behind!" She glanced at her watch. "I better be going. Look, Sue, I must put an advert in the paper by tomorrow lunchtime at the latest. Can you think it over and let me know in the morning? The flat's nice and we'll all look after you, help you sort yourself out. I don't mean to laugh at your problems, that's just my way, but I'll promise to stand by you, and try to understand."

She stood up. She had the creamy skin and rosy cheeks of a country girl and was popular with her colleagues because of her kindness and honesty. Sumitra got up, too, taking a deep breath. "It's O.K., Gwynneth," she said. "I've made up my mind. I'll take the room."

"Good for you, girl." Gwynneth smiled. "Betsy's moving out at the end of the month. You must come round one night to see the room and meet the others."

Every day for the next fortnight, Sumitra carried one of her dresses or skirts neatly folded in a carrier bag to work, and Gwynneth took the clothes home with her each night. By this method, and by wearing an extra jumper or T-shirt each day, Sumitra was able to remove most of her clothes from the wardrobe without arousing suspicion. She left some old garments hanging up, just in case anyone looked.

Now that she had finally decided to leave home, she felt calm and strong. She was patient with Ela and Bimla, helping them with their homework and buying them gifts. She was respectful and loving to Dadima and her parents, full of sympathy for them and wishing there were some other way to resolve the conflict.

She had long conversations with Sandya and realized that her sister was as concerned about the future as she was herself. "I don't know why you don't leave home," Sandya told her. "I'm sure I will when I'm eighteen." Sumitra almost confided the secret but managed to say nothing. It would be fairer for Sandya to be innocent, otherwise she would be punished for helping her older sister to escape. She longed to tell Maria, but knew she would be one of the first people approached for information about her whereabouts. It was best to implicate nobody and to regain contact after the move.

Legally, no one could stop her from leaving home, but in some ways her life would be ruined. She could expect no links with her family, and only ostracism from the more conservative elements of the Indian community. If Jayant found out where she was, she could envisage endless repeat performances of the pub drama. Mai and Bap would be round every night pleading for her return, and if she weakened and went back, nothing would have changed. They might possibly kidnap her, drug her, and send her to India. Farfetched as it sounded, it had been done before. If she remained at home, she would have to accept their laws. She could not accept them, therefore she had to leave.

Yet she dreaded the months ahead. It would be hard to take a leap into the unknown after a lifetime of having every major step marked out for her, of treading in other people's footprints. Now she would have to make her own footprints, and the thought terrified her.

Her last few days at home were full of a poignant sweetness. The pale winter sun poured through the French windows in the lounge, touching everything with a melancholy gold. The last time Dadima would scold her for wearing high heels. The last time she would make *chapatis*. The last time Ela would hide her lipstick. The last time Sandya would call her a silly cow. The last time Mai would tell her off for not having done the ironing.

Travelers have often remarked that the night before their departure all the annoyances that have irritated them over the previous months or years have seemed to disappear, as if someone had rubbed the scribbles off a beautiful painting. While they sat eating the last supper around the table that she had bought in one of Hanbury's sales, she felt the tears starting from behind her eyes. "Mai," said Ela, "Sumitra's crying." Then they were all around her, warm arms cuddling her, asking what was wrong, was she ill, what was up. "It's nothing," she answered, trying to smile.

Bap looked at her anxiously. He had lost the habit of looking at his daughters; there never seemed to be time these days. They were growing so big, even Ela was ten. "I will take you out on Sunday," he said. "You choose, anywhere you like."

"Can we come, too? Oh, please, Bap!" clamored Ela and Bimla.

"Quiet now!" ordered Mai. "Sumitra, go and rest. Watch the television with your father. Sandya, Bimla, help me wash up!"

Sumitra sat on the settee. Dadima sat beside her, nodding her head and smiling toothlessly. "You are a good girl," she said. "Don't worry, all will be well."

There had never been another evening like it, as long as she could remember. It was almost like the advertisement on telly—mother washing up, daughter sitting down and being cosseted. Mai brought her in a cup of hot milk. It *was* the television ad, apart from a few minor details! How could she leave now, when they had experienced that rare moment of family solidarity?

She went to bed that night full of anguish. Mai had made her another glass of hot milk, with a cinnamon stick floating in it, and patted her on the arm. It was still not too late to change her mind. Gwynneth would find another flatmate, and

Sumitra would pay the rent until she did. After all, the scene tomorrow would be terrible. She might, almost certainly would, be outcast, forbidden the help and love of the family unit, alone in a world that was often racist and prejudiced. To isolate herself, to be free, demanded a certain courage that Sumitra knew she lacked.

When she eventually fell asleep, it was to a Technicolor world of horror films. The sky was full of fireworks, all deviating from their programmed course, falling down to earth and burning her limbs. Banquo and his sons stretched out their hands to her in a never-ending line, then turned into Catherine Wheels and zoomed round and upward, out into space and eternity. Birungi performed cartwheels around the bodies of dead men hanging from mango trees.

She saw herself sitting beneath one of the mango trees from which fruit and corpses hung in equal profusion. Sally and Trupti were crouching beside her, listening as she read a story. The story was about a world peopled with dwarfs: black dwarfs, white dwarfs, yellow dwarfs, brown dwarfs. The dwarfs spent their lives creating new instruments of torture, new weapons of destruction for dwarfs of different colors and beliefs.

Then she heard the sound of running feet. Turning to protect the children, she saw the gang of thugs upon them, felt the blows, tasted the blood, heard them screaming, "Paki, Paki!"

The pillow was wet. The light from the lamppost shone comfortingly onto the ceiling. She felt for the radio and switched it on, grateful for the dispassionate voice of Alistair Cooke on the World Service. Wiping the sweat from her brow, a great sense of peace swept over her. She lay back on the bed. She had found the answer to her question; it had been lying in a corner of her brain for years. It didn't matter what color anyone was, what language they spoke, what job they did, where they lived. The only people to whom it did matter were the dwarfs, the stunted ones. It was time to grow up, to move on, not just for her but for the world.

CHAPTER XIX

The note she left propped up in her bedroom was short and explicit. "I will be O.K. I'll be in touch. Please don't worry about me. I do love you all, but please try to understand. I had to leave. I must lead my own life."

She closed the door behind her and took the small bag in her hand. It contained her nightclothes, radio, toothbrush and makeup. Anyone glancing at her would have seen a young, smartly dressed Indian girl going off to work. But behind the smooth face, beneath the careful makeup, was a woman making a small step into the unknown.

Sitting opposite a middle-aged man who was hiding behind a copy of the *Telegraph*, reading about guerrillas in Latin America, was an urban freedom fighter. And as the train followed its customary and prescribed route—East Finchley, Archway, Camden Town, Warren Street—Sumitra knew that when she stepped for the last time off the Northern Line, she would be stepping into a new life.